TROUBLE AT BRODIE CREEK

Sam Hanley, marshal of Brodie Creek, has resigned to marry and become a rancher. However, trouble hits town when the Thad Cross gang — all killers — arrive. To avert disaster the townsfolk want Hanley back as marshal, but Hanley only becomes involved when the Cross gang raid the bank and kidnap his new wife, Ellie. To rescue Ellie he must follow Cross to Hangman's Perch, an impregnable outlaw roost. Everything seems stacked against him — can Hanley win through?

BEN COADY

TROUBLE AT BRODIE CREEK

Complete and Unabridged

LINFORD
Leicester

First published in Great Britain in 2007 by
Robert Hale Limited
London

First Linford Edition
published 2008
by arrangement with
Robert Hale Limited
London

British Library CIP Data

Coady, Ben
Trouble at Brodie Creek.—Large print ed.—
Linford western library
1. Western stories
2. Large type books
I. Title
823.9′2 [F]

ISBN 978–1–84782–469–1

Published by
F. A. Thorpe (Publishing)
Anstey, Leicestershire

Set by Words & Graphics Ltd.
Anstey, Leicestershire
Printed and bound in Great Britain by
T. J. International Ltd., Padstow, Cornwall

This book is printed on acid-free paper

1

'This town will surely miss you, Sam.' The murmur of agreement that rippled through the crowd gathered in the town hall of Brodie Creek was proof positive that the words of the town council chairman found favour with the citizens whom Sam Hanley had protected as their marshal for nigh on ten years. 'And I'm sure that every man — '

'And woman!' Amy Saddler shouted out, a sentiment that got ringing endorsement from the women in the hall.

'And women,' said Henry Saddler, casting a mean eye his wife's way.

'Thought it might slip your mind, Henry,' Amy Saddler crowed.

'As if you'd let it, woman,' Saddler grumbled, much to the amusement of the gathering. 'Now, dang it, I've forgotten where I was.'

'Don't worry, Henry,' said Sam Hanley, smiling wryly. 'I get the drift.'

'When this town was just raw lumber, tents and wagons ten years ago, it could have gone two ways, I reckon. Back to sand and tumbleweed. Or Brodie Creek could have become the kind of roughhouse town that decent folk could not live in.

'But when you pinned on that star you've worn so proudly, Sam, Brodie Creek became a safe family town. You sure put legs under any hardcase who sought easy pickings round these parts.'

Loud applause greeted Henry Saddler's assessment of Sam Hanley's worth.

'Now, in a couple of hours you'll be handing over that star to . . . ' Saddler pointed to a man in the front row, 'Dan Cockrell, whose been under your wing — '

'For too darn long,' Cockrell joked, to much laughter.

'Oh, shush, Dan,' Saddler chuckled. 'It's only now that Sam has managed to dry all that wet behind your ears.'

While another bout of laughter ran its course, Sam Hanley looked to Ellie Johnson, who returned an adoring look to the man she would marry in a couple of hours' time and with whom she would then set out to build the finest ranch in all of Arizona.

She recalled a day three months previously when she had arrived in Brodie Creek, fresh from Boston where she had worked on a Boston newspaper as a reporter, ready to turn the Brodie Creek *Echo*, which she had started from scratch, into the finest newspaper in the West. And she reckoned that she would have, too, based on how far she had got in three months, had Sam Hanley not been in Brodie Creek to upset her plans in the nicest way. She had, one rainy night, listened to Sam rambling on about one day owning a ranch that would make his sons — and daughters, too, he had quickly added, when she had cocked a critical eyebrow — the proudest darn critters in Arizona.

'Won't you need a wife to have those sons and daughters, Sam,' she had joshed him.

Sam Hanley had laughed in the easy, musical way he did. But in that moment there was a spark lit between them. That night had been the first time he had called her Ellie; it had always been Miss Johnson before that. And she surely liked the sound of her name the way he said it, soft and tender.

'Seems you've got a plan, Marshal,' she'd said. 'But you wouldn't want to wait until your teeth are falling out along with your hair before you get to making it happen. Seems to me that you need another plan to get the plan you have up and running.'

'What the heck are you talking about?' he had asked.

'Well, will it be a wife or cows first?'

'You know, Ellie, you surely are a woman who cuts to the chase.'

'The way you tend to go round in circles, Marshal,' she said, 'that's what you'll need if you're ever to unpin that marshal's badge and do what you have a clear hankering to do.'

It was when Sam Hanley had looked at her in a new way, that Ellie realized how he might have interpreted her advice as an application for the post he was looking to fill. And, surprisingly, she being a woman who saw her future as the editor-in-chief of the newspaper with the biggest circulation in the West, the prospect of becoming Sam's wife did not seem as outrageously foolish as it might have done before that rainy night.

Nothing much happened for the next couple of weeks, until one day, bursting in the door of the newspaper office, his lips already silently rehearsing what he was going to say and ready to say it come what might, Sam had blurted out, 'I've been thinking about what you said, Ellie, when I had room in my head when I wasn't thinking of you, and if you want to build that darn ranch with me I'd be mighty pleased to have you along.'

'And I'd be mighty pleased to come along, Sam,' she had answered, her career as a newspaper woman having lost its lustre when compared to sharing Sam Hanley's future with him.

'You would?' he checked, as if he hadn't heard right.

'All we need to start with is a preacher, Sam.'

He had danced out of the *Echo*'s office, rushing along the boardwalk, stopping anyone who came his way to tell them that Ellie Johnson had agreed to be his wife.

'Sam, look out the window,' Henry Saddler invited, going to the window ahead of Hanley to look at a spanking new wagon parked outside the town hall, loaded up with furniture every bit as new. 'That's our gift to you and Ellie,' he said. 'And by the time you're ready to roll out of here this afternoon, it'll have brand new canvas on it to protect those goods.' Sam Hanley was not an emotional man, but right then his words of thanks would not come from a throat constricted by feelings that were welling up from deep inside him. 'This town wishes you and Ellie every good fortune, Sam,' Henry Saddler had concluded.

A rider going by, covered in the dust of hard riding, drew rein briefly to size up the wagon and its contents. His eyes came up to look at Sam and Henry Saddler at the town hall window. He tipped his hat and rode on. His next port of call was the saloon. Sam Hanley reckoned, judging by the evidence of a long trail ended, that the man would have a sand dry throat to ease.

'Now, all that needs doing is to clear you folk out of here while these fine ladies,' Saddler's hand swept out to a group of women in gingham overalls, led by Amy Saddler, 'get the place ready for a wedding reception.'

'Come here, honey,' Sam invited Ellie Johnson. 'Ain't that some stylish rig to be leaving Brodie Creek in.'

Ellie Johnson encircled his waist with her arms. 'I'd be glad to leave town with you on the rump of a mule, Sam,' she said quietly.

'Darn it, Ellie, you be careful, you hear,' Amy Saddler piped up. 'A spoiled man is a terrible burden — '

'How the heck would you know?' Henry Saddler chanted.

'You've got to train a man like you would a dog or cat,' Amy Saddler continued, ignoring her husband. 'Believe me,' her gaze fixed on Henry Saddler, 'an untrained man is a burden to himself and a downright nuisance to everyone else, but most of all his wife.'

Ellie laughed. 'I'll keep him in line, Amy. That I promise.'

'That's my girl,' Amy said. Turning her back to her husband she gave Ellie a broad wink, matched by an equally broad smile.

'Doggone!' Henry Saddler groaned. 'Another good man's about to bite the dust.'

'Shoo, the lot of you,' Amy said. 'We've,' she included the women with her, 'got work to do.'

Although there was a mile-wide grin fixed on Sam Hanley's face, there was a dark shadow in his grey eyes as he let his gaze wander to the saloon porch where the man had paused to roll a smoke.

'What is it, Sam?' Ellie enquired, sensing his unease.

'Nothing, honey,' he said, drawing her in to his arms. 'Nothing at all.'

But he wondered if that were so.

2

Dan Cockrell glanced in the shaving mirror on the wall behind the marshal's desk, and used the cuff of his shirt-sleeve to polish the star that Henry Saddler, in his official capacity as the chairman of the town council, had just pinned on him.

'You've got to swear on the Good Book, Dan,' Saddler reminded the new marshal of Brodie Creek. 'So let's do that right now, son,' he invited the man who was twelve years Hanley's junior. 'Place your hand on the Bible and say after me:

'I swear by Almighty God ... ' Repeating the oath after Henry Saddler, Dan Cockrell drew his wife and four year old son to his side, peacock proud. 'So help me God,' he finished the oath, resoundingly, and added, 'I hope that I'll wear this badge with even half the honour you did, Sam.'

'Do that, Dan, and you'll be a good marshal. And an even finer man,' Saddler said.

Leaving the marhsal's office for the last time, Ellie Johnson still wondered about Sam Hanley's unease. Her fear was that he was getting second thoughts about a future that he had seemed so committed to and so enthusiastic about, now that the reality of his not being marshal any more had hit home. 'Sam,' she brought him up short as they walked along the boardwalk, 'you're not having doubts about what we've planned, are you?'

'Doubts?' He sounded astonished by her question, which encouraged Ellie. 'What the heck put that idea into your pretty head, Ellie?'

'Well, it's just that since you saw that loaded-up wagon, you seem to be some place else all the time instead of here with me, Sam. I was wondering if the wagon brought home to you that you were finally leaving Brodie Creek on a journey — '

'That I've dreamed about, Ellie,' he interjected.

Ellie turned Sam to face her and fixed him with a steady gaze. 'The thing is, Sam, reality usually falls far short of the dream.'

'What are you saying?' he questioned. 'Have *you* changed your mind, Ellie?'

'No, I haven't, Sam.'

Sam drew her into his arms and kissed her passionately, so passionately that when he finished his kiss she was redder of cheek than an Irish leprechaun's hair.

'Change my mind?' Hanley chanted. 'I'm the luckiest damn man alive that you've agreed to be my wife, Ellie Johnson.'

'Sam Hanley,' she playfully rebuked him. 'Please remember that kissing like that comes after and not before the wedding! Now, I've got a last editorial to write. And I'm not sure that my mind can settle to it.' She blocked his way at the door of the newspaper office. 'And if you're going to hang around, I most definitely will not. Now, go!'

Sam Hanley chuckled.

'You're booting me out already, woman?'

'See you at three p.m. sharp in the church, Mr Hanley,' she said primly.

'Yes, ma'am,' he said, clicking his heels.

'Heh, don't forget something that will keep you in mind?' She pouted her lips. 'And,' she put her hand against his chest, 'not something that will have my hair standing on end when I stand before the preacher.'

This time Sam's kiss was gentler and strangely, for Ellie, all the more passionate. Breathless, she closed the door of the newspaper office.

As Sam made his way back to the marshal's office to clear up any outstanding paper work that had his mark on it, the man who had ridden in a short time before came from the saloon to lounge against a support beam of the porch overhang, his eyes travelling after Hanley as he progressed along the boardwalk, his scrutiny and interest getting all the keener as he turned into the marshal's office.

'What can I do for you, Sam?' Dan Cockrell enquired, hoping that Hanley was not the kind of man who thought no one else could do the job as good as he had, and therefore felt that he was obliged to offer a mountain of advice that he hoped would have the new man doing the job exactly as he had.

'Just some paper work that needs clearing up, Dan,' Hanley said.

'I can do that, Sam,' Cockrell said stiffly, taking umbrage at what he saw as Sam Hanley thinking that he was not up to the job in any way.

Recognizing in Cockrell's stance what had been in his when he had become the marshal of Brodie Creek and every wag in town had ideas as to how he should do things, Hanley had the good sense to back off.

'Of course you can, Dan. I don't

know what I'm doing here.'

Cockrell, who had learned his trade under Sam Hanley's guidance and had learned it well, did not miss the former marshal's frowning glance through the partly open door to a point that Cockrell reckoned would be in the region of the saloon.

'Something interesting you, Sam?' he asked, strolling to the door to join Hanley. 'Like that fella propping up the saloon porch, maybe?' When Hanley showed surprise, the new marshal grinned, 'You taught me well, Sam.' His grin faded and his face took on a sombre look. 'Trouble, you reckon?'

'Probably just another drifter passing through,' the former marshal opined.

'That's not really what you think, is it, Sam?'

'Well, there's something about his gait, Dan . . . '

'Like the way he wears that sixgun? Low and tied down.'

Hanley laughed. 'Couldn't have it flapping about on the trail. Might ruin his prospects with the ladies if it swung the wrong way.'

'Checked the dodgers in the drawer, Sam. Nothing. But I'll keep an eye on him.'

'You know, Dan,' Sam Hanley opened the office door fully to leave, 'I reckon that Brodie Creek has got itself a fine lawman.'

When Hanley closed the door, the perspiration that Dan Cockrell had been working so hard to keep in check now broke through every pore. And his scrutiny of the man lounging on the saloon porch had none of the nonchalance it had had when Sam Hanley was present. Rolling in on him, like a speeding locomotive, was the fact that he was now standing alone behind the marshal's badge and not backing Hanley's play. And never in his wildest imaginings had he realized the difference.

He returned again to the desk drawer and picked up the Wanted posters which had arrived in the mail a couple of days before. Hanley, by then winding down his role as marshal, had left the mail to him to attend to and therefore Sam had not seen the poster he was now looking at, with a shake in his hand. There was no mistaking that the man lounging on the saloon porch was the same as the man in the dodger, though he had hoped that it might not be. Thad Cross, wanted for murder, rape, bank robbery and a thousand other heinous crimes had grown a flourishing moustache, but there was no mistaking who the visitor to Brodie Creek was. There were three other dodgers which made up the Cross Gang, all with the same pedigree as Thad Cross. Two of the gang were relative newcomers. But Cross's long-time saddle partner, one Rupert Riddle, a Virginian, was his undoubted equal in his crimes, if not even more evil.

3

Passing back, on his way to the barber shop for a shave and a haircut and a bath in the fancy tub in the back room, Sam Hanley purposely crossed the street to bring him within spitting distance of the stranger who had, a short time before, ridden in. At a distance he was a threatening and ugly critter. However, the knife slash on his right cheek, from just under his eye to his jawline, added a new dimension to Hanley's first perception of the man. Of course, there was many a man in the West who, through no fault of his own, looked like Satan's brother. But Hanley had the distinct and very troubling feeling that the stranger had earned every ounce of the evil and menace he exuded.

'Howdy, mister,' Thad Cross greeted Hanley affably, as he went past.

'Howdy,' Hanley returned, reservedly.

'Nice town you got here.'

'Peaceful and trouble free,' the former marshal said, pointedly. 'The way we like it.'

Thad Cross grinned.

'Guess I'll have another go at slaking my thirst,' he said. 'Care to join me?'

'I've got a wedding to go to,' Hanley said, and continued on past.

'Be sure to give my regards to the bride and groom,' Cross called after him. 'You hear now, mister?'

Sam Hanley waved a hand in the air in acknowledgement.

'I won't refuse to join you, mister.'

Thad Cross spun round on the man tugging at his sleeve, his thirst stripping him of every last vestige of dignity. Cross's first reaction was to shove the drunk away as he might a mangy dog, but he changed his mind. Brodie Creek was the kind of town he figured would be easy pickings. So the information the drunk could give him in return for a bottle might be very valuable: information about the man who had just walked past. In his time he had learned that knowledge about a town made it a whole lot easier to control, and when that control was no longer needed, infinitely easier to depart from safely.

'Glad of the company, friend,' he said, putting an arm round the drunk, while at the same time wanting to rip his heart out for the stench that blocked his nostrils. 'Whiskey, OK?'

The drunk's eyes lit up like lamps in the dark.

'And while we sup, we can talk, huh?'

'Anything you say, mister,' the drunk gulped, his tongue licking parched lips in anticipation of the delights to come.

'Lived in this burg long, friend?'

'Come in on the first wagon,' the drunk boasted.

'So you know most folk round here?'

'Ev'ryone above and below ground.' He giggled, his gaze going to the bar.

'A bottle for me and my friend,' Cross ordered from the barkeep who, by the cocked-eyebrow look he gave Cross, was puzzled that anyone should want to have Brodie Creek's most notorious drunk for company. So astounded was he, that the barkeep was unable to hold his tongue.

'You lost your wits, mister. Wantin' to share a bottle with the town drunk.'

Thad Cross fully understood the barkeep's astonishment. The rest of the saloon's clientele obviously shared the barkeep's puzzlement. Cross, however, was anxious to get what information he could from the drunk, who, unlike anyone else he might question, after a bottle would not be able to recall anything he had asked. With the purpose of keeping the drunk sweet, Thad Cross leaned across the bar, grabbed the 'keep's shirt and hauled him across the bar.

'Mister,' he growled. 'My company is my business. And your business is to give me what I asked for without insulting my friend.'

Emboldened, the drunk stepped up

to the bar, shoulder to shoulder with Thad Cross. 'Just put the bottle on the bartop and mind your own damn business, Larry,' he told the barkeep.

The barkeep's reaction was predictable. 'I'm goin' to toss you out in the street where you belong, Barney Clements,' he bellowed, his fleshy face suffused by a rush of anger. He went to clear the bartop.

Cross shoved him back inside the bar.

'You throw my friend out, and you're going to have to sling me out with him.' Cross's right hand drifted to hover over his gun. 'Now, maybe you'd better think long and hard about that,' he advised.

The barkeep's Adam's apple bobbed, and fear haunted his muddy eyes.

'Now, I think you should apologize to my drinking-buddy,' Cross added.

The barkeep had had to perform tasks that had not settled well with him before but, by the spite in his mean eyes, Cross had handed him a task that he would almost prefer to die rejecting rather than complying with. And die he undoubtedly would, if he challenged the stranger's ultimatum.

'Maybe I was out of turn,' he muttered.

Thad Cross cupped his ear. 'You say something, barkeep.'

'I said that maybe I was out of turn,' the barkeep said a little louder.

Cross shook his head, and twigged his left ear with his fingers. 'Darn, I must be going deaf. I'm afraid you're going to have to shout, barkeep.'

The barkeep's temper was so intense that he almost passed out from the rush of blood racing up the back of his neck to explode in his head.

'Loud and clear,' Cross demanded.

'I said that maybe I was out of turn,' the barkeep shouted.

Thad Cross's grin was a fetching one, exercised mostly for tempting ladies to part eagerly with what they spent most of their time protecting. 'Now, that wasn't hard, was it?' Cross grabbed the bottle of rotgut off the bartop and, an arm round Clement's shoulders, went and sat at a table that was well out of earshot of the saloon's other imbibers.

'You told Larry good, mister.' Clements giggled.

Cross had no doubt that the barkeep would at some point in the future claim his pound of flesh for the humiliation visited on him. Clements would probably end up in an alley one dark night kicked to death. But for now all he could see was a full bottle. Thad Cross poured, filling the drunk's glass right to the rim. Clements sipped at the whiskey in a pretence of a man at ease with liquor. However, his restraint soon vanished and he gulped down the rotgut greedily. Cross refilled his glass instantly.

'You see that fella I exchanged greetings with a couple of minutes ago?' Cross asked. Clements nodded. 'Important fella in town, I reckon?'

'Used to be,' the drunk said. 'Ain't no more.'

'How come?'

'Used to be the Brodie Creek star-packer. But he's getting married and leaving town in a couple of hours.'

'Wears a gun like he can use it?'

Barney Clements nodded. 'Over the years, a lot of fellas found that out when they got on the wrong side of Sam Hanley.'

On hearing the name, Thad Cross tensed. Word of tough law was quickly communicated through the hardcase community. And the name Sam Hanley had come up frequently, when tough law was mentioned.

The drunk's eyes fixed on the bottle which Cross was protecting.

'So you've got a new badge-toter, huh?' Cross prompted Clements.

'Yeah.'

Cross poured a drink. 'You don't sound impressed, friend.'

'Dan Cockrell used to be Sam Hanley's deputy. I figure the step up is a step too much for him. Hah! Cockrell's all show and no darn substance.'

25

Pride shone in Barney Clements' rheumy eyes.

'I used to be Sam Hanley's deputy when he first pinned on a star,' he said proudly. He looked at the shaking hand holding the glass, and pride was overtaken by a deep and miserable shame. 'Long time ago now,' he said with a tired sigh. For a moment he considered putting down the half-consumed glass of whiskey but his resolve melted and, unable to resist his thirst a moment longer, he finished his drink in one long swallow and shoved his glass across the table, his eyes glazed and fixed on the bottle of rotgut. For a moment his befuddled brain misunderstood the smile on Thad Cross's face, expecting it to be friendly when it was mean.

'You know, fella,' Cross drawled. 'I figure the barkeep was right.' He put his hand over his mouth. 'It ain't proper for a man to be sharing your stinking company.' He turned the bottle upwards and let the whiskey out in a slow stream that spread across the table, following the grain of the wood. Cross enjoyed Clement's distress. 'Lick it up if you want it,' he taunted.

By now the drunk was the centre of amused and cruel attention as, with cupped hands, he tried to stop the whiskey from flowing off the table. After a minute of cruel goading, the laughter ceased suddenly and all eyes went beyond Thad Cross to the batwings behind him. The hardcase turned in his chair to see what had brought about such a dramatic change in the mood of the saloon.

Sam Hanley had turned back from the barber's shop.

'What'll it be, Marshal?' the barkeep piped up, suddenly busy with a bar cloth. 'Heh, but you ain't marshal no more.' The barkeep's mood of respect slipped, as did the mood of the other men in the saloon.

Sam Hanley looked sadly at Barney Clements, then his gaze switched to the man seated at the table with him, his mien one of outright insolence. He crossed quickly to the table where the drunk was frantically trying to stop the last drops of whiskey from dripping to the floor.

'Hello, Barney,' Hanley greeted the drunk, who looked up at him with an ocean of shame in his reddened eyes. 'Join me for a drink at the bar, friend.'

'Thanks, Sam,' said Clements, standing up on unsteady legs, trying desperately to overcome his thirst and leave with a modicum of dignity. 'Another time, huh?'

'Ain't much time left, Barney,' Hanley said. 'I'll be leaving town in a couple of hours.' He clapped his hands. 'Tell you what, Barney.' He went quickly to the bar. 'Give me a bottle.' The barkeep grudgingly obliged. Hanley gave the bottle to the drunk. 'Have that drink on me later.'

Clements took the bottle and held it close to him, a treasured possession. 'This town will be all the poorer for not having you around, Sam,' he said, and shuffled out.

'Who started this?' Hanley asked immediately the batwings had closed behind the drunk. 'You?' he quizzed Thad Cross, when the other men looked any place but in Cross's direction.

Cross nonchalantly raised his chair on its hind legs and began to roll a smoke. 'I guess it was me, sure enough,' he said, in a take-it-or-leave-it manner. 'Now what business would it be of yours, mister?'

Sam Hanley moved swiftly. His right boot kicked the chair from under Cross and he went sprawling on the floor. The hardcase's reaction was purely instinctive when he went for his gun. Hanley stood on Cross's wrist and applied pressure in increasing measure until Cross's fingers opened and the gun fell from his grasp. Hanley kicked it away. Then he hauled Cross to his feet, and in the same movement landed a brain-rattling blow to the side of his head that sent Cross reeling out of control across the saloon to crash painfully against the bar, scattering tables as he went. Hanley was standing over him when his eyes focused again.

'A man with a liquor problem is to be pitied instead of mocked and humiliated, mister,' Hanley said. 'Now haul yourself to your horse and hit the trail!'

Recovering his wits, Cross said, 'If you ain't the law round here no more, you've got no right to tell me to do anything.'

'That a fact?' Hanley crooned.

'That's a fact,' Cross growled.

'Give me your shotgun,' the former marshal ordered the barkeep.

'My blunderbuss?' the barkeep yelped. 'What for?'

'To pepper this gent's behind with buckshot if he's not on his horse and riding by the time I reach the count of three. Now give me the blaster!' he ordered when the barkeep dithered.

The barkeep handed over the shotgun.

'Use that and it would be plain murder, Marshal,' Cross said.

Sam Hanley snorted. 'But I ain't

marshal any more, friend. Now. One . . . Two . . . ' Thad Cross sprang to his feet. He paused for a moment to consider how serious Hanley was, and seeing no sign of play-acting on the former marshal's part he fled the saloon. 'Smart move,' Hanley said.

Cross paused in the batwings. 'I have a long memory, mister.'

'Good. Then you'll know that coming back to Brodie Creek wouldn't be a sensible thing to do,' the former badge-toter flung back.

Checking on Cross's departure at the window before giving his opinion, the barkeep said, 'I'm not sure that was a very smart thing to do, Hanley.'

Sam Hanley snorted. 'I've done dumb things before.'

'That fella's got an ocean of spite in him,' another man said. 'And ya know what worries me. When you're gone, that gent will come ridin' back to town to take his spite out on someone else.'

Another saloon imbiber was blunt and direct.

'You had no right to stir trouble for the rest of us, when you won't be 'round to finish what you started, Hanley.'

'Yeah,' another voice shouted. 'Ya should've remembered that you ain't the marshal of this burg no more.'

Sam Hanley recognized the veracity of all of the statements made, and also understood the speakers' fears for the future. There was no doubting the spite of the man he had ordered out of town, and neither did he doubt his potential for trouble. He had acted in the manner he would have done had he still been marshal, so conditioned had his responses become in the years he had toted a badge to dealing swiftly with any pending trouble. Sam Hanley looked around him at hostile faces.

'Ya should have left it to Dan Cockrell!' declared the angry man who had spoken last. 'He's the law in Brodie Creek now.'

'You're right,' Hanley told them

collectively. 'I stepped out of line, and I'm sorry.'

'Sorry ain't goin' to be much good, if that *hombre* comes back,' the barkeep said sourly.

4

On seeing the new jasper in town back out of the saloon, snarling, only a minute after Sam Hanley had entered Dan Cockrell started breathing even faster than he had been, and that had been pretty fast to begin with. The reason for the jasper's unceremonious departure was obvious — Hanley had run him out of town, and Cockrell reckoned that he knew why, too. A short time before (watching from the law office window the way he had been since the shock of having the responsibility for keeping law and order in Brodie Creek, rather than riding Sam Hanley's coat-tails, had registered with him), he had seen Barney Clements latch on to the jasper and had expected the man to give the drunk a quick shift, but instead, to his astonishment, the jasper had taken Clements under his wing. However, he reckoned that their association had turned sour just about the time that Sam Hanley had visited the saloon and, knowing the former marshal's pity for lame dogs like Barney, he must have taken exception to whatever treatment the jasper was handing out to the drunk. That was the only explanation for the events he had witnessed that he could come up with, because the jasper had been in town too short a time to have crossed Sam Hanley in any other way. And now his opinion was one that would be the equal of those expressed in the saloon.

His fears, too.

'Why didn't you mind your own damn business, Sam!' Cockrell fumed. 'Ain't right that you should hand me problems and then hightail it!'

Consumed by thoughts of trouble that might lie ahead, the new marshal did not notice the former lawman until he was almost looking him straight in the face. He pulled back from the window, but too late.

Outside, before he entered the marshal's office, Sam Hanley had been worried by what he had seen in Dan Cockrell's face — naked fear. Of all the men in Brodie Creek who could have pinned on the marshal's badge, he had reckoned that Dan Cockrell would be the most suited. But he should have realized that stepping up from deputy to marshal was a step beyond what many men were able to make. When trouble came a-calling in Western towns, it was the marshal's or sheriff's lot to deal with it. And though a deputy usually backed the marshal, the hardcases causing the ruckus always looked with a degree of pity on the second-string nature of a deputy. So much so that if the marshal called it wrong and paid the price, his deputy was often ignored.

'Howdy, Sam,' Cockrell greeted the former marshal cheerily, having hurried to seat himself behind his desk in as nonchalant a manner as he could manage. 'Thought by now you'd be all prettied up in your wedding-duds.' He chuckled. 'Ellie ain't got sense and ditched ya, has she?'

'Might be the sensible thing for her to do, Dan,' Hanley said, joining in the marshal's false banter.

'Well, you can't have your badge back, Sam,' he said jocularly.

'Don't know if I'd want it, now that I've finally got rid of it, Dan.' Sam drew in a deep breath. 'Funny thing, you know . . .'

'What is?'

' . . . The way I can breathe easier. Never realized how heavy that tin star was until I got it off my chest.'

Sam Hanley hoped that his admission, false though it was, would encourage Dan Cockrell to voice his own fears about wearing a star, and there was a brief second in which he might have, but he settled the mask of joviality and nonchalance quickly back in place. A man voicing his fears can often go a long way to overcoming them.

'Better than nursing cows, I reckon,' Cockrell said. Anxious to be rid of Hanley, because he was not sure of how long he could keep up his pretence of *bonhomie*, Cockrell shuffled the paper work on the desk. 'Will you just look at this mountain of paper I've got to get through!'

'It's surely a problem, and getting to be a bigger headache every day, Dan. Soon a lawman will have more need of reading and writing than of a fast draw.'

'Ain't that a fact?' Cockrell shuffled the papers on his desk again. 'Was there something you wanted, Sam?'

'Just dropped by to bring you up to date on happenings in the saloon,' Hanley said casually, though he was pretty sure that Cockrell had seen the incomer's swift and thunder-faced departure after he had put legs under him, and had put two and two together. He also figured that it was mainly his interpretation of those events and the possible longer-term consequences that had made Dan Cockrell so jittery. 'Had me a run in with that fella who rode in while we were all in the town hall.'

'Incomer?' Cockrell asked vaguely, shaking his head.

'Hung around on the saloon porch for a spell.'

Cockrell again shook his head. 'Can't say that I noticed, Sam.'

'How does wearing that badge feel, Dan?' Hanley enquired, considering the new marshal, who could not meet the former marshal's eyes for more than a couple of seconds.

'Don't know what you mean, Sam.'

'Well, it might be only a tin star, but sometimes it can weigh a ton and more, Dan.'

Cockrell acted the fool. 'Still don't know what you mean.' He polished the marshal's badge with the cuff of his shirt. 'It's resting real easy, Sam.'

'Glad to hear it, Dan. Now I've got to be moseying along, try out that new suit Moshe Cohen's made for me.'

'Saw you through Cohen's window last week when you were in for a fitting.' Cockrell laughed. 'Looked like one of those banker fellas.'

Sam Hanley frowned. 'I love Ellie dearly, Dan. But I sure would prefer if she took me in my everyday duds.'

'You're lucky a smart and good-looking woman likes of Ellie Johnson is having you at all, you ugly critter.'

'Yeah, I reckon I'm the luckiest fella who ever came down the line, Dan,' Hanley said with genuine warmth and wholesome honesty.

Dan Cockrell came from behind his desk to see Hanley out.

'Sam . . . '

'Yeah,' the former marshal prompted when Cockrell seemed stumped.

'Will you miss being a lawman, you reckon?'

'Too early to say, Dan,' was Hanley's honest reply. However, he figured that Dan Cockrell had not asked the question he had intended asking.

'I guess you won't. You'll be too busy having a brood of kids and nursing cows.'

Cockrell's mood was one of easy joshing, but Sam Hanley saw that his happy go lucky mood did not reach his eyes, and he became convinced that his former deputy, who had been so eager to step up to marshal, had become conscious of the onerous responsibility that was the difference between a deputy's star and a marshal's badge. And it worried him that his rashness in running the incomer out of town might rebound on Cockrell when he was no longer around to deal with the trouble his actions might visit on Brodie Creek and its new marshal.

He wondered if he should remain in town for a couple of days longer, until he was sure that the man had ridden on and was not coming back. But were he to do that, it would make Ellie hopping mad, and it would also undermine Dan Cockrell's standing as the marshal. And once that happened, Cockrell could wear a star for the rest of his days, but he'd never have respect.

Sam Hanley reckoned that over all,

moving on after the wedding was best for everyone; best for Ellie; best for him, and best for Dan Cockrell. Because he began to think that the answer to the question which Cockrell had raised about him regretting not wearing a badge, might be yes.

As he turned into Moshe Cohen's shop, preoccupied, Sam Hanley bumped into a tall man, pleasant of feature.

'Sorry,' he apologized. 'I wasn't looking where I was going.'

'Please, sir, you must accept *my* humble apologies. I, too, was not looking where I was going.' He tipped his hat and moved on.

Nice fella, Hanley thought. Even if he did not like a Virginia accent.

On entering Cohen's shop, the diminutive tailor was at the window, craning his neck. 'Hello, Samuel,' he greeted Hanley absently, his concentration on whatever or whoever he was watching, total.

The former marshal grimaced. No matter how many times he told the tailor to call him Sam, he still would not shorten his name.

'It's a good Biblical name, Samuel,' Cohen would say. 'Why would you want to be called Sam?' His astonishment at Hanley's repeated requests was truly genuine.

'Too much of a mouthful,' Hanley had given as the reason. But the real reason was that joshing folk had taken to calling him Samuel with comedic airs and graces. Hanley often wondered why his folks had not called him Hank or Ben or some other less joshable name. Hanley curbed his annoyance. In another couple of hours he'd be gone and the problem would no longer be a problem. 'Got that fancy cloth ready for me to step into?' The tailor waved an impatient hand. 'What the hell's so interesting, Moshe?' Curious, Sam joined the tailor at the window to see for himself what was so intensely preoccupying a man who normally went about his business and his life in a quiet, incurious way.

'That man,' Cohen said, pointing when there was no need to point, because the only man on the boardwalk between the tailor-shop and the bank further along the main street was the man into whom Hanley had bumped a minute before.

'What about him, Moshe? Seems like a gentlemanly sort of fella.'

Moshe Cohen shook his head vehemently. 'Bad man,' he said, and added emphatically, 'Very bad man, Samuel.'

The man graciously stepped aside to let two ladies pass, sweeping the hat from his head in a gesture of respectful homage that had the women looking admiringly after him as he continued on his way.

'I reckon you've read that gent wrong, Moshe,' Hanley opined.

Moshe Cohen shook his head even more vehemently. 'He is a killer.'

'A killer?' the former lawman questioned. 'A clean-cut fella like that?'

But of course he had crossed paths with clean-cut fellas before, who would cut their own mother's throat. But he saw nothing in this man to suggest the label the tailor had so adamantly put on him.

'I saw him kill a man in cold blood, Samuel. Shot him down for no other reason than it amused him to do so.'

Sam Hanley's study of the man intensified, searching for any hint in the man's gait or demeanour that would lend credence to Moshe Cohen's claim, and saw none.

'Reckon you called this one wrong, Moshe,' he said. 'Must look like this other jasper.'

'Moshe Cohen is not wrong!' he said with immense dignity. A small man, Cohen seemed suddenly taller as he drew himself up with the vehemency of his certainty. 'That is the man I saw in Langdon.'

'Langdon? That town died . . . oh, must be five years ago now. Nothing left now but tumbleweed and rotting buildings.'

'It died because bad men, like him,'

the tailor's finger pointed, 'made it a town where decent people could no longer live.' Cohen's gaze became wistful. 'At first Langdon was a nice town. I had a nice shop . . . '

'You had a needle-and-thread business in Langdon, Moshe?'

'Yes. Good business. Then men like that man came. Bad, evil men. Soon Langdon was a town where only an undertaker could do business. A place where only men like him could live.'

The man was crossing the street to the saloon. Moshe Cohen's adamancy had Sam Hanley looking with new interest at the man with the polite Virginia accent.

'This fella have a name?' he enquired of the tailor.

'His kind called him Rupert.'

'Second name?'

Moshe Cohen shook his head. 'I saw him murder the man the day I was leaving town, Samuel. Because, people said, the man called him Rupe. Why would a man murder another man for that reason, Samuel?'

'Because, my friend, some men don't like being called by their full monicker.'

'Monicker? What is this monicker you speak of, Samuel?'

'Name, Moshe. While other men,' he emphasized, 'don't like being called by anything but their full name.'

For a moment the tailor was confused, until the import of the former marshal's explantion registered with him. Then, excitedly: 'You mean the only reason he shot a man in cold blood was that he did not call him Rupert instead of Rupe?'

'That's about the size of it, Moshe,' Hanley confirmed.

'But that is not a reason for murder,' Cohen said.

'To some men it is,' the former marshal said darkly.

'Nonsense, Samuel!' Then, recalling what the former lawman had explained, the tailor added hastily, 'Sam.'

Sam Hanley laughed. 'Well, onc thing I have to thank our friend for, is you getting my name the way I like to hear it said, Moshe.' He shook his head. 'Now why didn't that fella make it to town a couple of years ago, and I needn't have worn out my darn tonsils trying to get you to call me Sam!'

'From now on, you are Sam,' the tailor assured him.

'From now on?' Hanley exclaimed. 'I'll be gone in a couple of hours.'

'Maybe that is as well, yes?' Moshe Cohen said, and then laughed. 'I get your suit now, Sam.' The tailor hurried away to his workshop behind the store.

Sam Hanley had known two or three men with Rupert as a handle, all of whom took exception to being called by their full dandyish name. There was only one man he had heard of who insisted on his full handle and took grave exception to it being abbreviated, a Virginian, called Rupert Riddle. A murdering bastard whom he had never set eyes on, but whose reputation for evil had reached to every corner of the West and beyond.

He watched Riddle swing into the saloon, with the easy gait of a man who reckoned that his match would not be found in the place he was in. And there was one other concern occupying Sam Hanley's mind, and that was the man who was an associate of Riddle; a man with whom he shared a common bond of murder and mayhem.

Thad Cross.

The former marshal of Brodie Creek now had no doubt at all that the scum he had run out of town was none other than Cross. Because where Cross went, Riddle tagged along. And vice versa. There was, he recalled, two other men in the Cross gang — apparently Thad Cross was a superstitious man whose lucky number, so it was said, was four. And therefore the Cross gang never went above or below that number. The men who rode with Cross and Riddle changed from time to time, of course, and it was not possible now to gauge their trouble-stirring natures. However, Hanley reckoned that if they were hired by Cross they would be the match of him, and every scintilla as poisonous.

Sam Hanley's attention was caught by Dan Cockrell coming from the marshal's office, his stare directed at the saloon. And even though the marshal's office was at the far end of the main street, well distant from Moshe Cohen's shop, there was no mistaking Cockrell's worry. Even though his face at that distance could not be read, his concern was in his gait, the droop of his shoulders, and the hand that went regularly to wipe away the perspiration from his brow. Dan Cockrell was a man who was mighty fretful. And it would take Riddle or Cross no time at all to sense his fear. In fact, so expert in assessing a man's degree of fear must Riddle be, that right now he must be picking up the scent of Cockrell's fear.

'This suit will be moth-eaten if you don't try it on soon, Sam.'

Hanley swung round from the

window. 'Sorry, Moshe. A man about to get married can get mighty distracted.'

Suit donned, the tailor circled Sam, checking every thread. 'Perfect,' was his proud verdict. Cohen gave one of his rare laughs, a rarity which was a pity, because his infectious laughter had a way of lifting a man's spirits. 'Not that I think the trousers will be staying on for long, eh, Sam?' Then, considering the former marshal with an air of melancholy, he said, 'Brodie Creek will miss you, Sam Hanley.' His glance went to the window to observe Rupert Riddle coming from the saloon to lounge on a porch rocker from which he dispossessed an old-timer.

'Dan Cockrell will make a fine marshal, Moshe,' Hanley said, feeling none of the inner confidence he had managed to put in his prediction.

The tailor's eyes travelled further along the street, and his conclusion was the opposite to Hanley's endorsement of the new marshal. 'Dan Cockrell is a good man, Sam. But . . . ' Cohen swung back to face Sam Hanley. 'Being a good man is not the same as being an able marshal.'

'Dan's been my deputy for over five years, Moshe,' Hanley exclaimed.

'That proves nothing, Sam, and you know it. I had an apprentice once, who was everything an apprentice should be, and he should have made a fine tailor. But the last I heard, he's still an apprentice and always will be. Abraham Goldstein just can't make the step up from apprentice to tailor, Sam.'

He returned his gaze to Dan Cockrell.

'Now I think that Dan Cockrell is like Abraham Goldstein. A fine deputy who will never make a fine marshal, Sam.'

Looking to Riddle, Sam Hanley observed the direction of the hardcase's gaze. And his cockiness told Sam that Riddle saw no reason for concern in the person of Brodie Creek's new marshal.

'Riddle is that feller's name, Moshe,' Sam said.

5

Patch Clark (so named because of the freckles covering his entire face except, for some extraordinary reason, a patch over his right eye) sprang off the bunk he was lying on and hurried to the window of the shack on hearing a rider approach. The rider being, as yet, unseen, Clark took precautions. He grabbed a rifle standing against a chair and readied it. He opened the window and stood at the side from which the rider would come into view, judging from the sound of his approach. He waited, ready to drop any unwelcome guest from his saddle the second he made an appearance.

He barked an order at the second man present who had taken up a position at the shack door, 'Cover the rear, Frank.'

'Ain't likely to be no one intendin' trouble, Patch,' Frank Bellows opined. 'Ridin' straight in the way he is.'

'Maybe he's real smart!' Clark snarled. 'Maybe he figures we'll think that way, while a coupla his partners circle round behind.'

'Never thought of that, Patch,' said Bellows, the fourth man in the Cross gang, with a look so dense that it reflected a brain that evolution had more or less passed by. He hurried away to the rear of the shack.

Clark caught a glimpse of the rider through a narrow break in the timber he was riding through, and almost risked a shot. However, being a cautious killer, Clark stifled the urge to take a risk that was not necessary. The rider's direction would, in seconds, bring him in to full view in a clearing where a couple of trees had fallen to a storm.

He raised the rifle, tracking the rider's progress, ready to down the man the second he got him in his sights.

'Got that fancy porcelain bath full of hot water, Sam,' said the town barber, coming to intercept Hanley as he went past on his way to the marshal's office, whither Dan Cockrell had retreated moments before under Riddle's sneering perusal.

'Put it on hold,' Hanley said, quickly going past.

'Doggone it, Sam. I just finished filling the tub. If you don't use it now, those pretty lilacs on it might fade. Noon, you said. Noon it is.'

'Not now!' Sam Hanley bellowed in an outburst that was at odds with his normally placid manner.

'Doggone, never knew a man to be so ornery gettin' married afore,' said the old-timer whom Riddle had dispossessed of the rocker outside of the saloon. 'Ain't like Sam to be that thorny. Looks kinda worried to me. And that ain't like Sam Hanley at all.'

'Surely ain't no ball of fun,' Riddle

observed, looking after the former marshal taking loping strides that ate up the boardwalk opposite.

Looking out the law office window, which he had done little else since he had pinned on the marshal's badge, Dan Cockrell had no doubt about Sam Hanley's destination. He quickly wiped the thick perspiration from his face and, as before when Sam had visited, he hurried to sit behind the desk looking busy. He fretted that Hanley, whom he knew to be a shrewd observer, would recognize in him the fear that was knotting every muscle and twanging every nerve-end raw. On the former marshal's last visit he had managed to keep his worry in check. However, since then, and particularly since Rupert Riddle had shown up, which told him that the Cross gang was not far away, his fear had mounted tenfold. And, this time, he might not be able to hide it as well as he had before.

In fact, it would take very little for him to beg Sam to take back his badge.

Or at least for him to remain around Brodie Creek until the Cross gang moved on. But doing either would make him, Dan Cockrell, a laughing-stock in town and for many miles beyond its boundaries. And were he to keep the marshal's badge (the town council might not let him because who the heck wanted a coward for a lawman), trouble would probably come calling every day in the form of hardcases who wanted to tease and torment Brodie Creek's yellow-bellied marshal.

The door of the marshal's office was flung open, almost causing Dan Cock-rell's heart to stop. 'Howdy, Sam.' He managed to greet Hanley brightly. 'Third visit in less than an hour. Homesick for the old place, huh?'

'Shelve the banter, Dan,' Hanley said. 'It doesn't convince me any.'

'What d'ya mean, Sam?'

'What I mean is, if you try and stand up right now, you'll topple right over on your face.' Hanley held up his hand to stay Cockrell's foolish protest. 'And the only thing of importance is, how do we deal with the Thad Cross gang?'

Cockrell's pride kicked in. 'It's none of your damn business, Sam! I'm the marshal of Brodie Creek now. And whatever needs doing, then I'll damn well do it!

'Now, ain't you got a bride waiting?'

★   ★   ★

The woman spoken of withdrew from the window of the newspaper office, deeply troubled by her future husband's constant visits to the marshal's office. She worried that Sam was regretting having handed in his badge and was finding every excuse and none at all to return to where he had amounted to something, possibly afraid of being nothing in the future. Ranching, as many men before him had discovered, was a hit and miss affair in which the transition from idea to fact was often a path of thorns. And Sam, at thirty-five, was not the oldest man ever to build a ranch from scratch, but neither was he the youngest. The West tired men quickly, used them up and then cruelly cast them aside. It took a special kind to take on the hardships and deprivations of the West on its own terms and succeed. She had thought Sam Hanley to be such a man.

But had she been wrong?

Ellie Johnson checked the wall clock. Three hours to her wedding, and she found herself wondering whether marrying Sam Hanley was the wise move she had thought it was. She loved Sam dearly, and it would break her heart not to have him as her husband. But what kind of a husband would Sam be if he was unhappy with his lot. Might marrying him be the unkindest thing she could do to him?

She saw Moshe Cohen come from his shop across the street. She hurried outside and intercepted the tailor as naturally as a hurrying woman could.

'Did the suit fit Sam OK, Moshe?'

she asked conversationally.

'Like a glove,' said the diminutive Jew. 'He'll cut a fine figure to be standing alongside, Ellie. Any nerves?'

'What's to be nervous about, Moshe. I'm marrying the man I love.'

'I hope you'll have fine sons.'

'And a daughter or two. An incomer?' She nodded in the direction of Rupert Riddle, hoping to discover what, if anything, had passed between the tailor and Sam when he had been in Cohen's shop for the fitting of his wedding-suit.

'One Brodie Creek could do without,' was Cohen's troubled response.

'Oh? He seems a gent.'

'That just shows how skilled he is at deception!'

'You know the man?'

'I know him,' the tailor said, shaking his head. 'And I wish I didn't. Stay well clear of him,' he counselled. 'That one's evil, Ellie. If I stood here for the next hundred years, I couldn't paint Rupert Riddle blacker than he already is. Satan himself is saintly compared to that gent.'

'Rupert Riddle, you say?'

'That's right. Heard of him?'

Ellie shook her head. 'Can't say that I have,' she lied, her heart knotted by the tailor's news. Not only had she heard of Riddle, but even if he had done only a tenth of the evil he was reputed to have done, Moshe Cohen's assertion that Satan would appear saintly compared to him was an opinion with a lot of merit. 'Has Sam heard of him?' she asked casually.

'Heard of him, yes. But hadn't set eyes on him until I pointed him out awhile ago. Knew Riddle from over in Langdon, before I set up shop here. He owns the blackest heart of any man, other than Thad Cross himself.'

'Thad Cross?'

'The man Sam ran out of town an hour ago, Ellie.'

'Sam ran Cross out of town?' she questioned the tailor. 'But why would he do that, Moshe. He's not the marshal any more.'

Moshe Cohen looked Ellie Johnson

61

straight in the eye.

'I'm not sure if Sam knows that, yet,' he said, and continued on along the street.

★ ★ ★

Patch Clark had the trigger of the Winchester squeezed to within a smidgen of full depression when he recognized the incoming rider as Thad Cross.

'Damn, Thad!' he swore. 'I could've plugged ya.'

'You're stupid enough, that's for sure!' the gang leader snarled.

Clark tensed, his face like thunder.

'No call for insults, Thad,' he growled. 'You're the one who told me and Frank to shoot on sight, if you didn't call out.'

Cross ignored Patch Clark's gripe. Swinging down from his horse, he asked, 'Riddle around?'

'Went to town.'

'I told everyone to stay put!' Cross

bellowed, his ire peaking dangerously. 'Until I came back with the lowdown on Brodie Creek.'

'Rupert figgered you was takin' way too long. Went to looksee, in case you'd gotten yourself in a bind,' Clark explained.

'Don't no one do what they're told?' Cross roared.

Frank Bellows came from the rear of the shack where Clark had sent him to cover the back of the crumbling structure. 'No call to chew us out, Thad,' he said. Normally a man who back-tracked rather than taking a stance, Bellow's spirited response took Clark by surprise, and positively stunned Cross. 'Me and Patch couldn't do nothin' to stop Riddle if he wanted to go to town.'

'I guess not,' Cross said, surlily, but with no menace.

'If you was hangin' round town, how come ya didn't see Riddle?' Clark enquired.

'Yeah,' Bellows addcd. 'It ain't like Brodie Creek's got so many places a feller could be to miss a man.'

'Musta been gone by the time Rupert blew in,' Thad Cross grumbled. He mounted the steps of the shack, his hat low over his right eye. But, Clark having the eye of an eagle, the swelling under the gang-leader's eye was not missed by him.

'That looks real sore, Thad,' Clark said, pointing. 'Trouble in town?'

'Nothing to lose sleep 'bout,' Cross growled, brushing past Clark into the shack.

'Sure looks like trouble to me, Patch,' Bellows opined. 'Whoever landed that haymaker on Thad is a man I'd want to give a wide berth to.'

'You and me, friend,' Clark said, thoughtfuly scratching the stubble on his chin, worry shading his muddy eyes.

'Looks to me like Brodie Creek could be a whole pile of trouble,' Bellows said. 'Maybe we should look for easier pickin's, Patch?'

Patch Clark troubled the stubble on his chin even more thoughtfully. 'You sayin' we should light out, Frank?'

'I ain't sure what I'm sayin',' Bellows replied honestly. 'Only one thing for sure that I do know . . . '

'What's that?'

'That I don't want to die in Brodie Creek, Patch,' he said sombrely.

6

Ellie Johnson returned to the newspaper office racked with doubt and gloomy of spirit on a day when she should have been full of hope for the new life she was about to embark on as Mrs Sam Hanley. The earlier good humour of the farewell to Sam had vanished, replaced by a brooding tension that draped her in a cloak of despair and foreboding. She went to the window, casting her eyes along the main street to the marshal's office where Sam still was. What could he possibly be doing there? He might only be jawing with Dan Cockrell, but she honestly did not think so. Because Sam's demeanour was not that of a man on a social call.

'Hello, Ellie.'

Startled by Harriet Scott's entrance, Ellie swung around. 'Last one,' she said, handing over the cookery tips copy she had been penning for the paper. 'I'll sure miss writing for the *Echo*.'

'Oh, I'm sure that in a short time another newspaper will open up in town, Harriet,' Ellie said, attempting light-heartedness, but failing.

'Nervous, huh?' Harriet Scott concluded. She laughed, and leaned close to Ellie to share a confidence. 'Natural. When I married Larry Scott, I near jittered myself to bits.' She shook her head regretfully. 'You know, this town won't be the same without Sam Hanley. Brodie Creek was a safe town with Sam as marshal.'

Harriet Scott glanced over her shoulder to check that no one had entered as stealthily as she had a moment before.

'Between you and me, Ellie. I reckon that Dan Cockrell, honest trier that he surely is, will fall a long way short of Sam's measure as the law in Brodie Creek.'

Ellie Johnson took the opportunity presented by Harriet Scott's praise of

Sam to raise the matter of the skirmish in the saloon earlier.

'Seems that new jasper who rode in made Barney Clements eat humble pie after he first befriended him. Sam took exception to his behaviour and ran him out of town, taking no nonsense, just like when he was marshal.'

Harriet Scott held Ellie Johnson's gaze.

'You figure Sam will be happy as a rancher, Ellie?'

'Of course he will, Harriet,' Ellie said positively. 'It's what Sam's always dreamed of.' Though her mood was upbeat, Ellie's heart was heavy. Harriet Scott had voiced the fears and doubts she had been fighting to contain, afraid to let them surface.

'Larry, rest his soul, used to say that lawmen are a special breed. That once he pinned it on, wearing a badge was something a man did for life.'

Was that true? Ellie Johnson wondered.

* * *

Dan Cockrell glowered at Sam Hanley. 'I'm marshal of Brodie Creek now, Sam. And I don't need your advice as to how I'll do my job.' The new marshal's reaction to Hanley's suggestion that he should run Rupert Riddle out of town with as much alacrity as he had Thad Cross was a thorny subject. 'Your time is past, Sam. Best that you get that through your head!'

Cockrell stood and drew himself up to his full six foot one inch height.

'The door is behind you, Sam.'

Sam Hanley knew that Cockrell's reaction was such that pushing his point of view any further would only rile the new marshal more than he already had been. And he also understood Cockrell's objection to his advice, because it mirrored his own response when he had pinned on a badge and everyone in town took every opportunity to offer their advice on what he should do and how he should do it.

'Sam.'

On hearing Ellie call his name from

the door of the newspaper office, Hanley shook himself free of his troubled thoughts. Riddle, still lounging on the saloon porch, let his gaze drift towards Ellie. 'Pretty woman,' he observed to a man hitching his horse to the saloon hitch rail.

'Finest in these parts, mister,' the man said. 'Sam Hanley is surely a lucky fella.'

'Sam Hanley?' Riddle's interest immediately perked up.

The man pointed. 'The fella crossing the street to the newspaper office. Getting hitched to Ellie Johnson in a coupla hours' time.'

Rupert Riddle smiled. 'Sure is a lucky gent indeed, friend.'

'This town won't be the same with Sam gone,' the man sighed. 'The finest and toughest lawman in these parts.'

He was telling Riddle something the Virginian already knew. He had heard tell of Hanley. And the stories told were of a man best avoided, if a fella was bent on trouble.

'Marshal of Brodie Creek for these past ten years.' The man's sigh deepened. 'But not any more. Got this loco idea that he'd like to be a rancher. Leaving town after he ties the knot.'

Riddle eased back in his chair.

'Pity,' he said. 'Good lawmen are hard to find.'

'Sure are, mister,' the man agreed.

Riddle waited a beat before eliciting the information he now needed. 'Got a new marshal, then?'

'Yeah. Fella by the name of Dan Cockrell. Used to be Sam Hanley's deputy.'

'Cut from the same cloth, huh?' Riddle enquired, as if his interest in the new marshal was simply passing.

'Remains to be seen,' the man said, sceptically.

'Seems you don't figure he is?'

'Oh, I guess Cockrell was dandy as Sam Hanley's back-up. But I'm not so sure that he'll be anyway near as good as Sam, fronting.'

'Maybe he'll have a good deputy, too?'

The man shook his head. 'No deputy. Brodie Creek is going through a lean patch. The town can't afford a deputy. In fact, if Sam was staying put, Cockrell would have been let go.'

'Times are tough all round,' Riddle sympathized.

'Brodie Creek will get back on its feet,' the man predicted confidently. 'But maybe it won't be the same town when it does, without Sam Hanley around to put legs under sidewinders.'

'Things can't be that bad. The bank's got plenty of customers coming and going.'

'You know banks, mister.' The man laughed. 'Even if there's not a spare dime to go round, banks still got bulging coffers.'

'Maybe you won't lose your marshal after all,' Rupert Riddle observed, directing the man's attention to Ellie in what appeared to be an angry exchange between her and Hanley.

'Oh, ain't nothing but fright.' The man chuckled. 'Recall when I was about to get hitched, I was as nervous as a man finding a rattler in his pants pocket. More sparks flew 'tween me and Lucy, my darling wife now, than would fall from a blacksmith's anvil.'

★ ★ ★

'That's darn nonsense, Ellie,' Sam Hanley said. 'I'm done as marshal of Brodie Creek.'

'Are you, Sam?' She challenged him. 'You're not acting like you've finished. Running Thad Cross out of town like you did. If you had concerns, you should have passed them on to Dan Cockrell.'

'You know who he is, then?'

'I know who he is and how dangerous he is,' Ellie stated. 'Where Riddle goes, Cross goes.'

'Then you also know how poorly equipped Dan Cockrell is to go up against an *hombre* of Cross's ilk, Ellie.'

'It's for Cockrell to decide on how *he* deals with Cross, Sam.'

'Cross was making a fool of Barney Clements,' Hanley stated curtly. 'Never did, nor never will stand for one man humiliating another, especially when that man can't help himself, like Barney.'

'Look at me,' she commanded. She drew him into the newspaper office. 'I don't want to spend my days tied to a man who wants to be some other place, doing some other thing.' She took his hands in hers. 'Sam, I love you dearly, and I hope you love me enough to do what we planned on doing — building the finest ranch in these parts, and raising kids to continue one day what we build. But,' she put her finger to Sam's lips as he was about to speak, 'if you've changed your mind, Sam I've got a newspaper to run instead.'

'I've never loved, and never will love any woman nearly as much as I love you, Ellie,' he declared fervently. 'And you're right, of course. I don't wear the marshal's badge in Brodie Creek any more.' Sam took Ellie in his arms and kissed her passionately. 'See you at the church in a couple of hours, honey.'

As he left the newspaper office he kissed her again.

'Looks like the wedding is on again,' Rupert Riddle murmured. He stood up, stretched, and strolled to where his horse was hitched, vaulted into the saddle and rode out of town, pausing only for a half-beat as he rode past Hanley to glance his way, his smile as close to mocking as did not matter. His pause further along the street outside the marshal's office from where Dan Cockrell appeared was a fraction longer, and his smile had gone from close to mocking to outright derision.

Cockrell made a brave effort to match look for look with the outlaw, but Riddle was the undoubted winner of the contest.

As he rode on, his shoulders shook with mocking laughter.

'Nice feller,' was the opinion of the man Riddle had been talking to outside the saloon. 'Took a real interest in our town. Wanted to know everything going on round here.'

'Did he ask about Sam Hanley, Arthur?' Cockrell asked.

'Yeah. Took a real interest in Sam, Dan. Told him all about the wedding and how he'd be leaving town.'

Cockrell vanished back inside the marshal's office, where he stood with his back to the door, his breath coming hard and fast, his legs threatening to buckle under him. He cursed the impulse that had sent him outside to make his mark by arresting the outlaw on the strength of the dodger he held on him. All he had done was make Riddle aware of his fear and weakness.

He thought about ripping the star from his shirt and walking out. However, he knew that he could not do that. Sarah, his wife, was the proudest woman in Brodie Creek that he had succeeded Sam Hanley; his kids, too, especially his eldest boy. If he walked out, he would go from shining knight to yellabelly, and all that would be left to do was skulk out of town with his tail between his legs. Besides, he was an honourable if fearful man who took his oath of office seriously. All he had to do was stand up to the Cross gang. If, by some miracle he slung them in jail or outgunned them, word would travel fast to others of their kind who would then give the town a wide berth as they had during Hanley's time, and his remaining years as the marshal of Brodie Creek would be a pleasant passage to a porch rocker.

'Stand up, Dan Cockrell,' he said breathlessly. 'That's all you have to do.'

He caught sight of his pale, sweating face in the shaving-mirror behind the desk, and a new hopelessness took him over.

Watching from the window of the newspaper office, Ellie Johnson had witnessed the interplay on the street, first between Rupert Riddle and Sam, an encounter of which she reckoned Sam had the edge, though slight. And then, further along the street, the exchange of glances between Riddle and Dan Cockrell, which undoubtedly, despite the new marshal's show of bravado, left Riddle untroubled.

Cockrell had come confidently from the law office, but had slunk back inside, and she knew that Sam was right. Dan Cockrell would come nowhere near to standing up to the Thad Cross gang.

Maybe, Cockrell thought, Riddle's departure from town was the last he would see of him or his cohorts, but it was a hope that was dashed as soon as it had sprung. Cross and Riddle were no fools. If their visit to Brodie Creek had been purely speculative at first, the sense of unease and uncertainty in the air now would attract them back, on sensing a town ripe for take-over. They would probably wait to return until Sam Hanley had left, because there had been no mistaking Riddle's concern as he had ridden past Sam. But as he had ridden by Dan, his manner made it obvious that he saw no threat in the new marshal.

'Howdy, Marshal.'

Cockrell spun round on hearing his wife's cheery greeting. 'What're you doing here?'

Taken aback and made to feel decidedly unwelcome by her husband's curt reaction, she meekly said, 'We've got a wedding to go to.'

'That's not for hours, Sarah.'

'Well, I thought we might go for a stroll, Dan.'

'A stroll? What for?'

'I'm proud of you, Dan. And I want to show off that shiny new star you're wearing. We often used to go for a stroll when you were Sam's deputy.'

His hand waved over the dodgers on his desk, still there after rooting out the Wanted posters on the Cross gang.

'Well, I ain't a deputy any longer. As marshal, I've got a whole mountain of paper work.' He picked up a handful of dodgers to emphasize the point, and when he slapped them back down on the desk the dodger on Rupert Riddle fluttered to the floor. Sarah picked it up to put it back on the desk, then hesitated on seeing the face on it.

'Wanted for rape and murder,' she read. Her eyes met her husband's. 'I'm sure I've just seen this man, Dan. Riding out of town just now'

'Couldn't be.'

'I'm pretty sure . . . '

'Last I heard, Riddle was hiding out in Mexico from a bevy of lawmen and bounty hunters on his tail,' Cockrell lied.

'Well, I guess I was mistaken then,' said Sarah. She placed the Wanted poster of Rupert Riddle with the others on the desk. 'I guess you're busy, honey. I'll drop by in about an hour.'

'Yeah. That should be about right to sort this lot out,' he said pleasantly. 'Sorry if I was a tad tetchy just now, Sarah. But,' he sighed, 'I never realized how much paper work went with the marshal's job.'

Sarah Cockrell paused before leaving, frowning worriedly. 'I'd have sworn on a stack of Bibles that the man in that poster is the same man who just rode out of town, Dan.'

'You'd be wrong, Sarah,' Cockrell insisted. 'Like I said, Riddle is hiding out in Mexico. Now,' he crossed to the door and opened it, 'don't you get wrinkles from fretting over nothing at all, you hear? See you in an hour, honey.'

Sarah Cockrell put a brave face on leaving, but as soon as she was out of sight worry took her over and she began to regret pushing her husband so hard in taking over the new marshal's badge from Sam Hanley. She had unwisely thought that life for the marshal of Brodie Creek would not change, but had foolishly not realized that it was not the badge that made a town safe, but rather the man it was pinned on. And though her husband was a fine and caring man whom she loved dearly, she had seen something in his eyes just now that, though he acted carefree, could not be completely hidden — fear. Of course Rupert Riddle and whoever he was riding with, would revisit Brodie Creek. Because like the animals they were, they would pick up the scent of Dan's fear.

Sarah Cockrell wanted to run back to the marshal's office and tell Dan that she understood, and that he could hand in his badge. However, were she to do that, it would probably do every bit as much damage to her husband as Riddle's bullet would.

It would just take longer for him to die.

''Morning, Sarah.'

She came up short. 'Sam. I thought you'd be all dolled up by now in that fine suit Moshe Cohen made for you.'

The former marshal laughed. 'Putting on a suit ain't natural to me, Sarah. So I guess about five minutes before the ceremony will do just fine.'

'You're as nervous as a newborn kitten, aren't you, Sam?'

'Rather face a passel of gunslicks than tying the knot, Sarah,' he confessed. 'I love Ellie dearly. And when the knot is finally tied, I'll leap over the moon with joy. But you've got to understand that a man giving up his freedom is bound to tremble some.'

The barber came from his shop.

'Marshal, are you taking that bath some time soon?'

'I ain't the marshal,' Hanley called back. 'Be seeing you at the festivities, Sarah.'

'Sam . . . '

Sam Hanley turned back. 'What is it, Sarah?' he prompted on seeing her hesitation.

'Oh, nothing, Sam. Don't drown in that bath.'

Hanley looked worriedly after Sarah Cockrell as she hurried away, and he knew that she, too, had come to realize that Dan Cockrell would be no match for the Cross bunch if . . . no, *when* they returned to town.

As she hurried away, Sarah Cockrell fought every instinct to turn back and, as she had intended, beg Sam Hanley to remain on in Brodie Creek until the threat from Riddle and his cohorts had been dealt with or had passed.

Having witnessed Sarah Cockrell's demeanour, Ellie Johnson had a good idea of what the new marshal's wife had in mind, and it filled her with a sense of foreboding that her plans for the future might be about to unravel.

7

Thad Cross, grim-faced and mean-tempered, came from the shack to glare at Rupert Riddle as he rode in. 'What's the big idea of disobeying my orders?' he challenged.

Riddle was untroubled by the gang-leader's rebuke, because he held all the cards in the deck. 'Figured that I'd have a look round Brodie Creek, Thad. Pity I didn't arrive before you left, huh?' His tone of voice conveyed the subtext of his message perfectly to Thad Cross, leaving the gang-leader in no doubt that he knew about his hasty and humiliating departure from Brodie Creek.

'Ah, nothing worth arguing about, I guess, Rupert,' Cross said in a carefree manner.

'Don't reckon so,' Riddle replied, smiling slyly.

Expecting fireworks between Cross

and Riddle, Patch Clark and Frank Bellows felt a keen sense of anticlimax at Cross's sudden and puzzling capitulation.

'Let's open a bottle,' Cross said, leading the way into the cabin.

'What the heck's all that about, Patch?' Bellows wondered.

'Beats me,' Patch Clark said. 'But,' licking parched lips, 'let's get us some of that liquor, huh?'

Imbibing over, Cross led the way from the cabin, Riddle strolling casually along behind him. Cross went and sat on the trunk of a storm-felled tree, still keeping up the pretence of goodfellowship. Checking that Clark and Bellows had not followed Cross said, his tone belligerent, 'Don't forget, Rupert. I'm still the boss of this outfit.'

'Never said you weren't, Thad,' Riddle replied, easy of manner. Rupert Riddle looked Cross squarely in the eye. 'Maybe after robbing the bank in Brodie Creek, we should ride separate trails, Thad.'

'Maybe we should at that,' Cross agreed. 'But I don't recall saying anything about robbing the bank at Brodie Creek.'

'We'll do it during the wedding shindig,' Riddle said, ignoring Cross's rebuke.

'You've got it all figured out, ain't you?'

'I do,' Riddle replied, in a tone inviting Cross to contradict his plans. 'I figure Patch and Frank will like a bank robbery that'll be as easy as taking candy from a baby.' The suggestion was a clear challenge to Thad Cross's leadership.

Cross knew that with Riddle backing them, Clark and Bellows would not hesitate to throw in their lot with the Virginian. Over the past couple of months Riddle had been slowly getting up the steam to take over. And his direct disobeying of his order to wait for his return from town was, Cross reckoned, an act of defiance to bring the question of leadership to the fore.

Well, he would not give Riddle the chance, this time.

'Robbing the Brodie Creek bank sounds like a good idea, Rupert,' he said amiably, enjoying Riddle's astonishment.

'Glad you approve, Thad,' the Virginian said, quickly overcoming his surprise at Cross's slick turning of the tables.

'Fellas,' Cross hailed Clark and Bellows. 'Come join Rupert and me. We've got us a great idea.'

* * *

'Now what the heck will you want that for?' asked Mame Brown, his landlady for the past ten years, when she saw Sam Hanley come downstairs wearing his gunbelt. She laughed in her high-pitched way. 'You won't need to force Ellie Johnson to the altar. She's been wanting to get you there ever since she set eyes on you.'

'I'd feel naked without the rig, Mame. It ain't left my hip in a long time.'

'Well it sure will today,' Mame said, trying to unbuckle the gunbelt.

'Leave it be, Mame,' Hanley said curtly.

Surprised, because Sam Hanley was the most courteous of men, Mame Brown stepped back. 'Sure, Sam. If that's what you want.'

It was not what he wanted. But if trouble came acalling, which he was pretty certain it would, he wanted to be ready to respond.

★　★　★

Mounted and ready to ride, Rupert Riddle said, 'Figure we'll get an invite to the nuptials in Brodie Creek, fellas?'

'Let's ride,' Cross said, his tone brusque, when Clark and Bellows laughed at the outrageous idea.

Thad Cross was forming a plan in his head to solve the problem of the gang's leadership. Rupert Riddle had a plan too, but his plan had not come in the last couple of minutes. It had matured back in Brodie Creek when he had seen Sam Hanley and Ellie Johnson together outside the newspaper office.

8

'Do you, Sam Hanley, take this woman to be your lawful wedded wife to love and cherish for all the days of your life?' The Reverend Clinton's rich mellifluous voice rolled over the congregation, which consisted of most of the town. Expecting an immediate response, the preacher was taken aback when Sam Hanley looked at him vaguely and dithered.

Ellie Johnson was even more surprised by Sam's hesitation.

The congregation, puzzled by their former marshal's apparent misgivings, held its collective breath. The marriage of Sam Hanley to Ellie Johnson was the most welcome development in Brodie Creek for quite a spell. Was it now to fall flat?

The women in the congregation were feeling sorry for Ellie. While the men, figuring that if Sam Hanley had changed his mind, he was the most loco critter in the territory.

'Sam?' said the Reverend Clinton, gently prompting Hanley. 'You've got to say 'I do'.' Then, aware of how he might be unfairly coercing the former marshal into a marriage he might have changed his mind about, added, 'That is, of course, if you want to?'

Sam Hanley, suddenly aware of the absolute stillness in the church, came to realize the reason for it. 'Sure I do, Reverend.' Then: 'I do,' he said loudly and clearly.

Though Sam Hanley's declaration was now positive and whole-hearted, Ellie Johnson could not help wonder why it had taken so long for Sam to give it.

'Are you really sure, Sam?' she whispered.

'I'm sure, Ellie,' he said, softly.

'That's good enough for me,' Ellie said, on seeing the blaze of love in Sam Hanley's eyes.

The Reverend Clinton relaxed, as did the congregation.

'Well, then, Ellie. Do you take Sam Hanley — '

'I do, Reverend.'

'Then I pronounce you man and wife. You may kiss the bride, Sam.'

Sam Hanley took Ellie in his arms and kissed her until she was breathless.

'Hope you've got something left for the honeymoon, Sam,' Henry Saddler called out, earning a deep furrowed frown from the Reverend Clinton; a frown that deepened further on hearing the laughter that followed Saddler's joshing, before the preacher, like everyone else, joined in the good-natured banter.

'Now give the woman a chance to draw her breath, Sam,' Clinton said, stepping between him and Ellie when Sam drew her to him once more.

However, there was one man in the congregation not laughing — Dan Cockrell. And it was Hanley's preoccupation with the troubled marshal that had caused his lapse of concentration. And it worried Sam also that Sarah Cockrell's fretfulness was an indication that she had, like him, reached the conclusion that if trouble visited Brodie Creek in the form of the Thad Cross gang, her husband would either be killed or shame himself by running away.

So, she would be widowed or married to a coward.

Ellie Hanley saw her husband's gaze go Cockrell's way, and she was full of trepidation at the thought that Sam would be dragged into something that was no longer his business, because he had a caring nature.

'First man to the town hall gets a bottle to himself,' Henry Saddler declared. The rush from the church was both ungainly and ungodly.

'Henry Saddler, you're doing the devil's work,' the Reverend Clinton rebuked him.

'It's pure Kentucky rye, Reverend,' Saddler said, a mischievous gleam in his eye, knowing well the preacher's fondness for good liquor.

'Well, I suppose we should be getting along at that,' Josiah Clinton said, ushering the newly-weds quickly out of the church. 'Don't want to keep folk waiting.' At the church door he paused and looked back and crossed himself, seeking forgiveness before the sin.

Outside the church, Dan Cockrell was leaning against the hitch rail rolling a smoke, his fifth. The four previous attempts had been wasted by fingers that refused to co-operate. The fifth was likely to follow suit.

'Ain't you in the race for that free bottle, Dan?' Saddler enquired.

'Ain't a whiskey-drinking man, Henry,' he replied with a grin, the warmth of which made no impression on his cold and troubled eyes. 'Be along shortly.' He caught Sam Hanley's eye, but quickly looked away, knowing that Sam was reading him like an open book.

'If we don't hurry, Sam,' Ellie said, 'there'll be nothing left to eat or drink.'

As they got into the rig that Henry Saddler had provided for the bride and groom, Sam glanced back. Dan Cockrell's gaze was fixed on the road leading into town, his every muscle tensed. He was dragging on a smoke that was coming apart. He flung it away angrily.

'You don't wear a star any more, Sam,' Ellie said quietly.

'Let's get this shindig over with and shake off the dust of this town, Ellie,' he said, hugging her to him.

'If you like we can leave right now, Sam.'

'That would be discourteous, wife. You wouldn't want Brodie Creek thinking badly of us once we're gone, would you?'

He flicked the reins to start the rig rolling.

★　★　★

'Well?' Thad Cross asked Patch Clark after he climbed back down the tree from which he had been observing the happenings in Brodie Creek.

'Looks like the only one who ain't gone to the weddin' is the marshal, Thad.' He chuckled. 'Looks like he's right off his food and liquor right now.'

'We'll wait a spell before we ride in.'

'Why wait?' Rupert Riddle wanted to know. 'That shivering marshal won't give any trouble.'

'An hour from now and most of the men will have had a skinful. But right now, they might just take to shooting at bank-robbers.'

'I reckon that makes a whole pile of sense, Rupert,' Frank Bellows said.

Patch Clark was quick to back Cross's plan, too. Riddle thought about pushing his point of view, but instead went along. His anxiety to reach Brodie Creek was driven by something other than robbing the bank.

The damn bank would not be going anywhere.

'That's settled then,' Cross said. Dismounting, he wondered what Rupert

97

Riddle, not a man given to anxiety, was so anxious about? Then, like a bolt out of the blue, the answer came to him. And now that he knew, Riddle was not going to have it all his own way.

9

'Aren't you coming to the wedding, Dan?'

Dan Cockrell turned to greet his wife Sarah. 'Sure I am, honey. In a little while.'

'It'll be over. Ellie is anxious to be away as soon as possible. She wants to make it to Clover Ridge before nightfall.'

'Don't see the sense of leaving and just going ten miles. Why not wait and start out at sun-up?'

'What woman would want her honeymoon night on her own doorstep.'

'Can't see that it makes a whole lot of difference,' he said, impatiently returning to his perusal of the road into Brodie Creek. 'We started our honeymoon under your pa's roof, remember.'

Even in the tense atmosphere, Sarah laughed on recalling her first night as

Mrs Dan Cockrell. 'How could I forget? Every time we moved the bed creaked. As I recall, at breakfast you were unable to look my pa in the eye.'

Cockrell laughed along with her, but his moment of levity was brief, before his troubles piled in on him again and once more his gaze returned to where it had been steadily for over an hour.

'You go back to the festivities, Sarah,' he said glumly. 'I'll be along in a little while.'

'You know, you could be worrying about nothing, Dan,' said Sarah Cockrell quietly, glancing about her to make sure that there was no one around to hear.

'Worried?' said the marshal, airily. 'What have I got to worry about, Sarah?'

Losing her patience Sarah said sharply, 'The men who were in town earlier. The Thad Cross gang. They're probably long gone.' She looked about at the signs of a town suffering hard times. 'There's nothing much in Brodie

Creek to make them want to stay.'

She looked her husband straight in the eye.

'There's nothing much for anyone to stay for, Dan. We could move on, too.'

'Move on?' he scoffed. 'Brodie Creek will come back. All towns go through rough patches.'

'There's nothing much to keep us here. We could follow in Sam and Ellie's footsteps. Calder Flats is booming, and it's only fifty miles from here. No distance at all, Dan.'

'We're staying put,' he said stubbornly. 'Like I said, Brodie Creek *will* come back.' Looking beyond Sarah, the marshal's features set in stone on seeing Sam Hanley looking their way from outside the town hall. 'What's wrong with him?' he snarled. Sarah swung around. 'Everywhere I've looked today, Sam Hanley's been looking back at me.'

'I guess he's worried, too, Dan.'

'What's he got to be worried about?'

'You, of course,' Sarah snapped, her patience having run out of leash. 'He's worried that the Cross gang will return and that you'll — ' Sarah bit her tongue.

'That I'll what, Sarah?' Cockrell asked quietly. 'Turn tail, is that it?' He came face to face with Sarah. 'Is that what you think, too?' His eyes took in every inch of Brodie Creek. 'Is that what everyone thinks?'

'There's no shame in asking for help, Dan,' Sarah pleaded. 'Sam Hanley would have.'

His shoulders slumped despondently. 'Sam never needed anyone's help, Sarah.'

'I'm sure Sam would stay around for a couple of days, if you asked him to.'

'I'm not asking.'

'Dan, I don't want to be a widow.'

'What makes you think you will be?'

'You're not Sam Hanley, Dan,' Sarah stated bluntly, feeling that the time for straight talking had come. 'You're not as fast or as accurate with a gun to begin with.'

'Sam never found me wanting!'

'Being deputy to Sam Hanley meant that all you had to do was tidy up when Sam had finished. And there was little enough of that to do, because hardcases like Cross and his partners gave Brodie Creek a wide berth when Sam was marshal.'

'Thanks for the vote of confidence, Sarah,' Cockrell said bitterly.

'Straight talking was needed, Dan.' She came close to him, but he stepped back to re-establish the gap between them. The hurt in Sarah Cockrell's eyes went deep. 'I love you, Dan Cockrell, every dumb and stubborn inch of you. And I'm darn sure that I wouldn't look good in black!'

She reached out to touch him on the arm.

'Don't throw away your life out of stupid pride, Dan. Please don't do that. Let Sam help. I know he gladly will.'

'Ellie might have something to say about that, Sarah. Sam's no longer a free agent.' The glimmer of hope which Sarah had when her husband's attitude softened for a moment was cruelly dashed. 'I'm not going to crawl to Sam Hanley or any other man in Brodie Creek for help, Sarah.

'If the Cross outfit come back, I'll deal with them my own way. Now, you go on back to the celebrations.'

He turned away from her, his stance uncompromising.

'Never thought I married a fool, Dan,' Sarah said, hurrying away.

★ ★ ★

'Climb that tree again,' Thad Cross ordered Patch Clark. 'It's been almost an hour. See what's happening.'

Clark's monkeylike ascent of the tree belied his clumsy and cumbersome appearance.

'Climbs trees like a darn ape,' Rupert Riddle observed, his tone indicative of how lowly he reckoned Clark to be in the order of things.

'Well?' Cross called out.

'That lawman's still keeping watch,

Thad. Don't seem to be 'nother soul 'round.'

'The marshal ain't no problem,' Frank Bellows opined. 'We can just cut him down.'

'And have the whole town on our backs,' Cross barked. 'Stick to muscle work, Bellows. Brains you ain't got.'

Anger, only a smidgen away from defiance, flared in Frank Bellows's eyes at the insult. Riddle was pleased, because he reckoned that Thad Cross's unthinking outburst had, should he choose to act, put Bellows firmly in his camp — Clark, too, by association. Because Bellows and Clark had become firm friends since Cross had recruited them.

Patch Clark climbed down from the tree and pointedly stood alongside Frank Bellows. The purpose of his action was not lost on Cross, and he understood the stupidity of his rash outburst. But he was confident that robbing the Brodie Creek bank and sharing its spoils would, for the present, occupy everyone. And after the robbery he intended to at least reduce the number of men to share with. And maybe, if he was really clever and really fast, the entire pot would be his. Along with the other prize he had in mind: a prize every bit as important as the takings from the Brodie Creek bank. Maybe, he considered, even more important. There were lots of banks to rob, but few women as desirable as the former marshal's new wife to possess.

'Can you still throw a knife the way you used to, Rupert?' Cross asked.

'Take the eye out of a fly at fifty paces, Thad,' the Virginian replied confidently.

'Then let's get along and see if you're still as good as you say you are,' Cross said.

*　*　*

'Dan's still being mule-stubborn, huh, Sarah?' Sarah Cockrell came up short, her breath caught in her throat. 'Step in here.' Sarah did as Sam requested, and joined him in the recessed door of the general store.

'I don't know what you're talking about, Sam,' she responded, with wide-eyed innocence.

Hanley held her gaze. 'Sarah, I ain't a fool. And you ain't a good enough actress,' he said.

Sarah Cockrell dropped all pretence of innocence. 'Stubborn as ten mules. Dan's scared, Sam,' she admitted frankly.

'Ain't nothing wrong with being scared, Sarah,' Hanley replied comfortingly. 'There were plenty times when I wanted to turn tail, too.'

'You?' Sarah Cockrell was stunned by the former marshal's frank admission. 'The fearless Sam Hanley, scared?'

'Sometimes being scared gives you an edge. Makes a fella more alert. Nothing as dumb as a man who always thinks that there's nothing to be scared of all the time, Sarah.' He sighed. 'The trick is not to let the other fella know that you're scared.' He looked along the street to where Dan Cockrell was still wearing out his eyes watching the road into town. 'Trouble is, Dan ain't learned that trick yet.'

'Never had a need to when he was backing you, Sam.' She studied Sam Hanley. 'Thing is, there's no time left for Dan to learn that lesson, is there? Those men will ride back into town soon, won't they?'

'I figure,' Hanley said.

'And Dan will try and stand up to them, won't he?'

'I reckon.'

Tears welled up in Sarah Cockrell's blue eyes. 'And those men will kill him, Sam.'

Sam Hanley did not answer her question. Because had he, he would have had to lie.

'Will you help him, Sam?' Sarah Cockrell pleaded.

'I've tried. But the last thing Dan will accept is my help, Sarah.'

'Talk to Dan again, Sam. Make him

see sense. It's all this damn pride! You fellas would rather be killed and leave a widow behind than swallow it.'

'If Dan backs off it won't take long for word to get out. And then he'll be finished, Sarah. Besides,' his mood became darkly dour, 'Cross will murder Dan anyway. So I reckon that Dan might figure that pulling back will only send him to the next life marked as a coward. And he'll be counting, like most men in his kind of fix, that luck will favour him and postpone the Grim Reaper's visit until another day.'

'All I want is Dan to be alive after this, Sam,' Sarah said tearfully. 'You see, without Dan, there's nothing left.'

'I'll talk to Dan again. That's all I can do, Sarah. I can't force him to do anything. He's the law in Brodie Creek now.'

'Then, Sam Hanley, I'll be a widow before this day is through.' Sarah Cockrell turned and walked away, her shoulders shaking with her weeping.

Ellie Hanley had come from the

wedding reception looking for her husband, and had no trouble in guessing what he and Sarah Cockrell were tallking about when she saw them together, their glances going every now and then to Cockrell at the far end of the main street, still keeping a lookout for the trouble that was now in the leaden air over Brodie Creek to materialize.

10

Sam Hanley did as he had promised Sarah Cockrell. On hearing him approach, Cockrell swung around, his hand diving for his sixgun. Up close, Hanley could smell the fear coming from the new marshal. He tried to reholster his gun as nonchalantly as possible, but failed. A shaking hand has difficulty in smoothness of action.

'Ellie ain't kicked you out already has she, Sam?' he joked, trying desperately to stop himself from turning round immediately to renew his watch of the trail into town.

'We've been saving liquor and grub for you, Dan. If you don't come along soon — '

'Weddings ain't my bailiwick, Sam.'

'You got married yourself.'

'Well, that was one wedding I couldn't avoid. Never been to one

111

since, and don't intend to ever be. No offence intended of course, Sam.'

'None taken, Dan.' Hanley leaned on the church hitch rail alongside Cockrell. 'Smoke?' he asked, as he took the makings from his vest-pocket.

The craving for the weed was evident in Cockrell's eyes as he watched Sam roll the smoke.

'Trying to quit,' he lied. 'Sarah ain't too keen on the habit.'

When he fired up and the smoke drifted Cockrell's way, he craned his neck to savour its scent. Sam rolled another smoke and offered it to Cockrell, joking, 'Sarah ain't around, Dan.'

Laughing, the marshal eagerly took the smoke. Leaning back and dragging deeply, he observed, 'Cloud coming. You'll have to be making tracks shortly, Sam, if you and Ellie are to make it to Clover Ridge before nightfall. Dangerous travelling with a woman alone at night.'

Sam looked to the sky, which had, in

the last hour or so, become dark and moody — the kind of sky that depresses a man's spirits, and then gets even darker and moodier still on picking up his despondency.

'Dan,' Hanley began in a measured tone of voice, 'facing four with four ain't nothing to be ashamed of. In fact, I would say that it's the mark of a wise man.'

Cockrell glared, dropped the smoke and drove it into the ground with the heel of his boot. 'Are you saying that I'm scared, Sam?'

'Well, aren't you?' was Hanley's blunt response, seeing no point in pussyfooting any longer, as he reckoned that if Thad Cross and his hardcases were to put in an appearance, that appearance could not be far off. 'I've just been telling Sarah about the times I was scared, and scared good at that.'

Dan Cockrell was astonished.

'I can count at least twenty times when what I wanted most was to run.'

'You were a damn rock, Sam.'

'And I was also telling Sarah just

now, that the real trick in being scared is not to let it show. But that can be real hard to do.'

'Looks like you and Sarah had a real cosy chat, Sam,' Cockrell growled. 'She tell you I was scared? Well, it ain't true.'

'Have sense, Dan. Get help!'

'I'm real busy, Sam. And you've got a wife you should be attending to.' Cockrell turned his back to mark the end of their conversation.

'Don't be a fool, Dan,' the former marshal counselled. 'Boot Hill is full of fools.'

Cockrell walked off a couple of paces to emphasize the rejection both of the former marshal's counsel and of his company.

'If you don't round up a couple of deputies, I will, Dan,' was Sam's fierily delivered parting shot.

*　*　*

Watching from behind a nearby derelict building which had once been the town's hotel, before the slump in the fortunes of Brodie Creek had forced its closure, Thad Cross and his partners had been privy to the conversation between Cockrell and Hanley. At the time Riddle had suggested a more circuitous route to town, rather than riding straight in, Cross had thought that the Virginian's caution was a waste of time.

'There'll be no one in Brodie Creek who'll be in any shape to make a stand,' had been the gang-leader's prediction. 'So why waste time taking a wide circle?'

'There's one man who'll make a stand,' had been Rupert Riddle's counter argument.

'That frettin' deputy?' Frank Bellows questioned sceptically. 'He'll run faster than a jackrabbit, Rupert.'

'I reckon so too,' Patch Clark said.

Clark and Bellows were ignorant of the man Riddle had spoken of, but the Virginian's message was not lost on Thad Cross.

'Ya know, fellas,' Cross drawled, 'we've got lots of time. Let's do as Rupert says.'

'Doggone, Thad,' Clark grumbled. 'All this caution is givin' me a terrible headache.'

'So would a bullet in your skull!' Cross flung back, sulkily.

Now, lurking at the side of the derelict hotel, Cross had much to be grateful to Riddle for. Because eavesdropping on the parleying between Sam Hanley and Dan Cockrell had made him aware of the marshal's fear, and the former marshal's plans to organize the help which Cockrell was loath and stupid not to seek.

'Looks like this was a real good idea, Rupert,' Bellows complimented Riddle.

'We'd better move fast,' Patch Clark said. 'Before there'll be more lead in the air round this burg than there was at Gettysburg.'

'I've got a plan,' Riddle said.

'What kinda plan?' Clark asked.

'I'm the boss of this outfit,' Thad

116

Cross grated. 'Any planning will be mine to do.'

Patch Clark and Frank Bellows exchanged glances, and agreed on their course of action. Bellows said boldly, 'Rupert got it right this time, Thad. Patch and me see no harm in listenin' to this plan of his.'

Cross was of a mind to fix the rebellion, as he did most things, by slinging lead at those who did not see things his way. Riddle had, in his snake-oil way, in essence taken over the gang. But, firstly, shooting would be heard and only add weight to the former marshal's argument for rein-forcements. But, more important, there was a bank to be robbed. Once that had been done, there would be time to deal with Riddle.

It burned a hole in his gut to give ground, but Cross said affably, 'I guess you have a point at that, gents.' He invited Riddle, 'So tell us what this plan is, Rupert.'

'Sure, Thad,' the Virginian agreed,

matching Cross's affability, but fully aware that the gang-leader was not happy with the humble pie he had had to eat. But it did not matter. As far as he was concerned, in a short while from now Cross would be wormbait. 'I figure that paying a visit to this wedding party to take a hostage will let us rob the bank in peace and ride out of Brodie Creek sucking air.'

'That's the kind of plan I like,' Frank Bellows crooned.

'But first, we deal with the shaking marshal,' Riddle said.

* * *

Sarah Cockrell looked anxiously at Sam Hanley as he returned from his unfruitful attempt to get Dan Cockrell to see the insanity of standing alone against a quartet of killers such as the Thad Cross gang. His return glance could offer her no hope, and she fled the town hall before her hoplessness would spoil the wedding celebration.

Ellie Hanley tried desperately to be polite and understanding, but her worry for Sam, should he get involved with Cockrell's problems, and her own frustration and disappointment at having her wedding-day spoiled by Sam's regular disappearances from her side, made her best efforts at understanding difficult.

'I must be the most abandoned bride in the West, Sam,' she snapped.

'Sorry, honey. But Sarah asked me to try and get Dan to see sense and swear in a couple of deputies.' He spoke in a whisper, not wanting to spread alarm among his guests. 'You can understand how she's fretting, can't you?'

Ellie Hanley saw how unimportant her annoyance was compared to Sarah Cockrell's problems. Sarah had two young boys who could, if the Cross gang showed up, and if Dan Cockrell let his pride overrule his good sense, be orphans and she a widow.

'Yes, Sam,' Ellie said quietly. 'I can understand. I've got exactly the same worry as Sarah, you see. You're going to stand with Cockrell, aren't you?'

Ellie's smile was one of sad resignation.

'Sure you are, Sam. You were going to do so since the second you found out who the incomers were, and you knew that Cockrell would not be their match.'

'You have every right to be as mad as hell, Ellie,' he said. 'But I just can't let Dan Cockrell be gunned down.'

'You'll always be a lawman, won't you, Sam.'

'I've given up my badge, Ellie,' he protested.

'The law is in your blood, Sam. You're not wearing a badge. But inside, where it really counts, you're still Marshal Sam Hanley. Always will be, I guess.'

Hanley held Ellie's gaze.

'I'm not sure of what you're saying, Ellie,' he said.

'Neither am I, Sam.' She sighed disconsolately. 'Neither am I.'

Henry Saddler, a moderate drinking man, was still sober enough to understand that all was not well between the newly-weds. Moshe Cohen enlightened him.

'The Thad Cross gang?' he checked with the town tailor.

'The man Sam Hanley ran out of town was Cross. And the man who spent an hour or more sitting on the saloon porch was Rupert Riddle.'

Henry Saddler paled. 'They're out-and-out killers, Moshe. If they ride back into town . . . ' He shook his head in some trepidation, his concern obvious for his wife Amy in his worried glance in her direction.

'Maybe they'll ride on,' said the town tailor.

'If Sam was still the marshal, they probably would,' was Saddler's opinion. 'But they'll know that Dan Cockrell ain't up to the task, Moshe.'

'I saw Sam talking to Sarah Cockrell a while back, Henry. Then he went and talked to Cockrell. But it looks like, whatever advice Sam had to offer, Cockrell wasn't interested.'

'I've got to talk to Sam.' Henry Saddler hurried away.

'Henry's bearing down,' Ellie Hanley said, on seeing the town council chairman's determined drive through the wedding guests. 'And I'd say that he's just learned of the threat to the town, Sam.'

Sam Hanley looked round. But when he turned back, Ellie had disappeared.

'Sam.' Saddler grabbed him by the arm to forestall his going to search for Ellie. He beckoned to his wife to join them. 'Amy, go find Ellie. See if she's all right.'

'What's happening, Sam?' Amy Saddler enquired. 'Everything's OK between you and Ellie, ain't it?' Her concern was that of a good friend, and held no note of curiosity.

'Not now, Amy,' Saddler said. 'Go find Ellie. Go on,' he urged when she was inclined to dally. When she departed, Saddler concentrated his full attention on Hanley. The wedding-guests were by now becoming curious about the air of tension which had dampened the festivities. 'Cockrell will fold when he sees the Cross gang, I reckon, Sam,' he said.

'Damn. Who else knows about the Cross outfit?'

'Not many, yet. But,' his gaze swept the gathering, 'I figure that that won't be for long.' He came straight to the point. 'You've got to pin your badge back on, Sam.'

'I'm through with being a lawman, Henry.'

'Tomorrow, you can be. But right now, your pinning on a marshal's badge is the only hope this town's got. I'll go talk to Ellie. Tell her how it is. She'll understand, Sam.'

'What if I fall to Cross's lead, Henry? Ellie will have been a bride and a widow all in the one day.'

'Fall to Cross's lead?' He snorted, as if the idea was as remote as the moon. 'They wouldn't be riding back in here if you were still the marshal, Sam. And when they find out that you are, they'll turn tail, of that I'm sure.'

'Thanks for the vote of confidence, Henry. But even if Ellie agreed to my pinning on a badge again, temporarily, and she would have to agree,' he emphasized, 'I wouldn't be the same man.'

'What? Not the same man? What're you talking about, Sam?'

'I have a wife to think about, Henry. That changes a man. That fact will not be lost on the Cross outfit. And that's why I say, even with me toting a badge, that they may not be as ready to give Brodie Creek a wide berth, as you think.'

He looked an increasingly desperate Saddler in the eye.

'I'll tell you what I told Dan Cockrell. Swear in three or four shotgun-toting deputies.'

'What's happening?' Hanley and Saddler turned to the man who had asked the question. 'Something's happened. So don't try to fob me off.'

'Why's Cockrell been watching the

road into town for over an hour now?' another man asked.

'And why have you spent more time away from your bride than with her, Sam?' a third man questioned.

'Darn, I know,' the first man said, his eyes bright with recall. 'I knew I saw him some place before. It was over in Langdon on a visit to Moshe's shop over there.' He swung around, his eyes seeking out Moshe Cohen. 'You were at the door of your shop that day, Moshe when that fella who was lounging on the saloon porch gunned a man down 'cause he used the short version of his name — Rupe, he called him. My God, that fella is Rupert Riddle, ain't he?'

He swung back to Sam Hanley.

'And I'm guessing that the gent you ran out of town, Sam, is none other than Thad Cross.' Foreboding immediately gripped the wedding-guests. ''Cause wherever Riddle is, Cross is close by and vice versa.'

'Thad Cross?' a woman shrieked. 'He's an out-and-out killer!'

'Now all that toing and froing between Sam and Cockrell makes sense,' said the man who had caused the panic. 'You're expecting the Cross gang to come to town, ain't you, Sam?'

Instant panic raced throughout the wedding-guests and some fled.

'There's no guarantee that they will,' Sam Hanley called above the excited chatter that had broken out.

'They wouldn't, if you were the marshal, Sam,' another man maintained.

'That's what I've been telling Sam,' said Henry Saddler.

An instant chorus for Sam to take back his badge broke out.

'I'm not the marshal, and I don't want to be,' Hanley said. 'I've made my decision, and I'm leaving town with Ellie as we planned.'

'Never thought I'd see Sam Hanley turn yella.'

Sam swung round and landed a jaw-buster on the man who had spoken, sending him reeling back against the wall. The man, a beefy specimen, regained his feet quickly and squared off to Hanley. Henry Saddler stepped between the men.

'Fighting among ourselves is not going to help,' he declared.

Both men continued to eye each other for a while longer, before Sam Hanley dropped his challenge. 'Henry is right. Now, like I said, what I'd recommend is that some of you men volunteer to see the Cross gang off, if they arrive in the first place'

'We ain't gun-handy, Sam.' The town blacksmith had spoken, and his statement was fully endorsed by the other men present.

'I'll tote one shotgun,' Henry Saddler said.

'No, Henry,' Amy Saddler pleaded. 'You've got eyes that don't see good any more to begin with. And you've got rheumatism in your hands, too.'

'Has anyone seen Dan?' All present turned on hearing Sarah Cockrell's desperate enquiry. 'He's not on the street any more, Sam.'

11

Sam Hanley was about to rush to the door of the town hall to check on Sarah Cockrell's statement, when Patch Clark and Frank Bellows appeared, supporting a heavily bleeding Dan Cockrell between them. 'Howdy, folks,' Clark said. 'Seems your marshal got in the way of Mr Riddle's knife.'

Sarah Cockrell screamed and ran to her barely conscious husband. Bellows shoved her away. She tumbled backwards and would have fallen heavily had Sam Hanley not caught her.

'You got a doc in town?' Bellows enquired.

'He's had to go to Bush Creek to deliver a baby,' Saddler replied.

'Well, in that case, I guess the marshal's out of luck.'

The duo dropped Cockrell on the floor.

'What kind of animals are you?' Amy Saddler rebuked the hardcases.

'I'd keep a civil tongue, ma'am, if I was you,' Patch Clark growled. 'Me and Frank don't take kindly to mouthy women. Ain't that so, Frank?'

'Sure is, Patch.'

'Easy, Amy,' Henry Saddler advised his wife anxiously.

'Oh, fiddly!' Amy shrugged off her husband's restraining hand. 'I'm going to help the marshal as best I know how, and to hell with these toerags.'

Amy marched to where Dan Cockrell lay, moaning. Sarah quickly joined her.

'I'll carry Dan to Doc's infirmary,' Sam Hanley offered.

'No one's goin' nowhere!' Clark growled.

Hanley picked the wounded lawman up in his arms. 'Shoot me in the back if you want to,' he said. 'I guess that's what you do most of the time.'

Clark's hand shot out to stay Bellows's draw.

'Folks,' he said in a homely fashion.

'Right now Mr Cross and Mr Riddle are helping themselves to what's in the bank safe. And there'll be no trouble for you fine people if you just let them get on with their business. But if you don't . . . Well, that would be most unfortunate for everyone. Your name be Hanley?' he enquired of Sam.

'That it is,' Sam confirmed.

'Well, don't you get up to no tricks now.' He sniggered. 'Riddle likes to cut pretty women, ya see. And that newspaper lady is real pretty.'

Sam Hanley blanched. 'Riddle has Ellie?'

'Yeah, he's got her. Figured that if there was to be trouble in this burg, you'd be the most likely to start it. So Riddle figured that some insurance would be necessary to . . . well, make you see sense.'

'The marshal needs to have that wound cleaned and dressed,' Amy Saddler said. 'Doc's got what's needed in the infirmary. And I aim to go and get it.'

Amy Saddler swept past Clark, who had again to stay Bellows's hand. 'Don't hold with killin' no woman, Frank,' he growled. 'Your man?' He indicated Henry Saddler. Amy Saddler nodded. 'You get back here pronto, and no tricks. Or else your man gets lead in the heart, ma'am.'

'I'll be back before you know I'm gone,' Amy Saddler said, and added a promise. 'No tricks.'

★   ★   ★

On hearing the door of the newspaper office open, Ellie Hanley had come running downstairs to greet and forgive her husband, having had regrets about walking out of the reception the second her temper had cooled.

'Sam, honey,' she called out. 'I'm sorry. This town has been your home for a long time and of course you'll have to do all you can to help.' She burst through the door which led from the hall to the office and came up short

131

on seeing Thad Cross and, behind him, Rupert Riddle. Recognizing the peril she was in, she tried to retreat, but Riddle sprang between her and the door and kicked it shut. 'What do you want?' Ellie demanded, in as commanding a tone as she could. But there was no hiding the tremor of fear in her voice.

'Well, right now me and Rupert would like you to come along to the bank with us,' said Thad Cross. His laughter was as close to a hyena's as could be. 'Ya see, we're making a withdrawal.'

Riddle came up close behind Ellie, his breath coming hard. 'You're our insurance against anyone who might think that they don't like their bank being heisted. Fellas like your new-pin husband.'

He sniffed at Ellie.

Cross bristled at Riddle's antics.

'You smell real nice, ma'am.'

'We've got a bank to rob,' Cross growled bad-temperedly. 'Let's go!'

132

'Oh, my, ma'am,' the Virginian hardcase scoffed. 'I do think that Mr Cross is getting jealous of our little dalliance.'

'Get your filthy person away from me,' Ellie snapped.

Riddle maintained his equanimity. 'There'll be time later.' He stalked past Cross to the door of the newspaper office. 'Well, what's keeping you, Thad?' Waspishly, he flung open the door.

'I'm not going anywhere,' Ellie said, bravely defiant.

Cross grabbed her by the arm. 'Shut up and just do as you're told.' He shoved her ahead of him.

Patch Clark was at the door of the town hall when Cross came from the newspaper office, a gun poking Ellie's side. 'Let the man see, Frank,' he called back inside. Bellows stood back from blocking Sam Hanley's path. The former marshal barged to the door, alarmed and angry on seeing Cross and Riddle escort Ellie to the bank.

'Harm a hair of her head and I'll kill

everyone of you, so help me God,' Sam called out, only too conscious of how impotent his threat was, unarmed as he was (Clark had relieved him of his gunbelt) and under threat from Bellows's and Clark's cocked guns.

Riddle kicked in the door of the bank. Distraught, Charles Armstrong, the bank president, pushed his way out of the town hall to protest. Bellows shot him point blank.

'Anyone else will get the same!' he promised.

'You got the banker at that shindig, Hanley?' Cross called out.

'Your dumbhead partner just shot him,' Hanley replied.

'You shot the damn banker, Bellows?' Cross raged.

'How was I suppose to know he was the banker in this burg, Thad?'

'How the hell are we going to open the safe now, Rupert?' Cross worried. 'We ain't got nothing to blow the safe with. And we could be searching for the key to that box 'til hell freezes over.'

'Keep your hair on,' Riddle said. 'Patch, find the bank-teller.'

'What the hell good is the teller going to be?' Cross argued.

'You heard,' Patch Clark said. 'Teller, step forward.' Clark and Bellows scanned the crowd. 'Point him out,' he ordered the man nearest to him.

The man licked lips as dry as desert sand.

'Don't know who the teller is, mister.'

'Don't know, huh?' Clark fumed. 'You live in this town and don't know who the bank-teller is, huh.'

'I live outside of town. Don't have any business with the bank.'

Clark swept his gun across the man's face, shattering his jaw. He fell to his knees, howling. 'I hate whinin'.' He blew the top of the man's head off. 'Now, who's goin' to point out the teller, folks?'

Everyone crowded back into a corner of the town hall.

'There was no call for that,' Sam Hanley said.

'If I get impatient my trigger finger gets jerky, you see,' Clark said. 'Now, I'll ask you folk again to point out the bank-teller. And if you don't, I'll kill someone every second you stay quiet.'

'That's him,' one of the women screamed, pointing to an elderly man who was paler than a ghost.

'You the teller?' Clark checked. The terrified man nodded. 'Now that was easy, wasn't it? Get over here.' When the man shuffled over, Clark bundled him through the door. 'We got the teller, Rupert.'

'Nice and old,' Riddle observed to Cross. 'Been with the bank since it opened, I figure. That means that he's a trusted employee. So I'm counting on him knowing where the key to the safe is kept. Come join us, teller,' he invited.

The bank-teller shuffled along. Bellows fired a couple of shots into the boardwalk close to him. The elderly teller began a stumbling run which amused Clark and Bellows.

'Howdy, friend,' Riddle greeted the

teller. 'Now, we've got this little problem that I reckon you'll be able to solve.'

'Anything you want, mister,' the teller whined. 'Only don't kill me.'

'Sure won't,' Riddle said, placing an arm round the teller's shoulders. 'You're a very valuable man, teller.' He drew the teller with him into the bank. 'You see, with the banker dead, we figure that you'll know where he kept the key of the safe hidden.'

The teller's steps faltered and his eyes flashed wildly.

Riddle grinned. 'Figured right, didn't I? Now all you've got to do is open the safe. Then you can walk right out of here.'

'Sure?'

Riddle crossed his heart. 'Promise.'

'Don't do it, Stan,' Ellie Hanley pleaded. 'He'll kill you anyway.'

'Why, Mrs Hanley, ma'am,' Riddle exclaimed. 'I'm a southern gent, and a southern gent's word is his bond.' He turned to the bank-teller. 'The second the door of the safe swings open, you can leave.'

'He's lying, Stan.'

Thad Cross struck Ellie across the face. The blow flung her across the bank. 'I told you to shut your mouth,' he raged.

'I don't have a choice, Ellie,' the teller said. 'You know that Mary isn't well, and who'll take care of her if I'm not around. This way.' He went through to the bank president's office, and crossed to the far wall. Cross dragged Ellie along with him. The teller hesitated, and sought Rupert Riddle's assurance again.

'I gave you my word, teller.'

The teller reached up on the wall and pressed a spot on it. A section of the wall slid open to reveal a secret nook from which the teller took the safe-key.

'Clever,' Riddle commented. 'Like you said, Thad, we'd have been here until hell froze over before we'd have found it.'

'Open the safe,' Cross commanded the teller.

The teller, having done as he had been asked to do, looked to Riddle. 'Can I go now, mister?'

'Of course you can, teller. I'm a man of my word.' Relieved, the teller hurried from the office and reached the door before Cross shot him in the back. 'Thing is, teller,' Riddle sighed. 'Mr Cross ain't got no word at all.' He bent down to look into the safe. 'Ain't the biggest haul we ever got,' he said. 'But it ain't the worst either, Thad.'

'That's real good to hear, Rupert,' Cross said, turning from having shot the teller. 'But you won't need a dime where you're going.'

Sensing danger, Riddle turned quickly, but not quickly enough. He rolled his eyes up to try and see the hole in his forehead, before falling forward on to his face.

Ellie Hanley screamed at the top of her lungs.

12

Following on the gunfire from the bank, Ellie's scream froze Sam Hanley's heart. When Thad Cross came from the bank, using Ellie as a shield against any surprises that might be waiting outside, his relief just to see Ellie alive was palpable, even though she was still in Cross's clutches and in great danger.

'Thad,' Patch Clark called out, 'where's Rupert?'

'He tried to kill me and take everything for himself, Patch.'

'Yeah?' There was a note of doubt in Frank Bellows's voice.

'Tell 'em that's how it was.' Cross prodded Ellie with his sixgun. 'Or you'll die right now.' He called out to his partners. 'Ask the woman.'

'Ma'am?' Bellows hollered.

'It's as he says,' Ellie said, hating the lie but seeing no point in sacrificing her life for trash like the Cross hardcases.

'You've got what you want, Cross,' Sam Hanley said. 'Let my wife go.'

'Sure will, Hanley,' he said. 'Just as soon as me and the boys are clear of town.'

With a sinking heart, Hanley knew that Cross was lying and had no intention of releasing Ellie. He reckoned that Ellie was just as much of a prize as the bank loot Cross was clutching. His frustration peaking, he tried to wrestle Bellows's gun from him. But Patch Clark, ever watchful and alert for the slightest hint of trouble, reacted swiftly to come to the assistance of the slower-witted Bellows. He elbowed Hanley in the face. The force of the blow drove him back against the wall. Enraged, the former marshal immediately sprang forward again, but came up against Clark's cocked sixgun.

'I should kill you, mister,' Clark fumed. 'But we've got what we come for.' He sneered. 'The money and the woman. And I guess you sittin' here thinkin' about what's happenin' to your wife will be a worse punishment than any bullet could inflict.'

Frank Bellows sniggered.

'Ain't goin' to be much sleep nights for a spell, eh, Patch?'

'You fellas coming?' Thad Cross called out.

'Right away, Thad,' Clark replied, striding forward with Bellows at his heels, walking backwards to cover Sam Hanley.

Ellie Hanley sensed Thad Cross's growing tension as the gap between him and his cohorts narrowed, and she guessed the reason for his edginess. It was the murder in the outlaw's black heart.

'He's going to kill you!' she shouted at Clark.

The truth of what Ellie claimed was confirmed by Cross as he shoved her aside to get a clear shot. Clark, a second too late in reacting, felt the gangleader's bullet rip through his chest, shredding flesh and bone. The gaping hole that was blasted in his back allowed room for his shattered heart to exit from the wound in shredded pieces.

Frank Bellows got off a shot, but the shake of terror in his hand sent the bullet whining harmlessly wide of Cross. Cross's second shot did to Bellows what his first round had done to Patch Clark.

'Hold it!' he shouted, and trained his pistol on Ellie, who had tried to escape. Ellie came up short. 'Anyone who's got ideas can just forget them. Or the woman dies right now.'

Cross's eyes swept the gathering overflowing from the town hall for any sign of trouble. Satisfied that there would be none, he ordered Ellie to get on board Rupert Riddle's horse, hitched to the rail outside the newspaper office. Then he vaulted into the saddle and immediately raced out of town, dragging Ellie's horse along by the reins.

Sam Hanley immediately ran to the law office, buckled on a gunbelt and got a rifle. He vaulted in to the saddle of the first horse available and thundered after Cross. Even in the minutes that it had taken Hanley to arm himself the outlaw had opened up a sizeable lead, leaving the former marshal with little chance of closing the gap between him and Cross before they reached the foothills of the mountains south of Brodie Creek where, in a maze of trails (a lot of which were used by Cross's own kind to keep out of sight from curious eyes), Cross could take a long time to find: time during which Ellie could suffer horrors that would leave her scarred for life.

High in the mountains there was an outlaw roost, and it was there that Hanley figured Cross was making for. The roost, called Hangman's Perch, was a virtual fortress, the entrance of which was between twin ridges from where most of the country below could be viewed, making it impossible for lawmen to breach its security. A constant watch was kept by men who, if the new arrival was not known to them, had to see a Wanted poster as evidence of his right to the roost's hospitality and protection.

One smart lawman had once come up with the idea of having a dodger printed with his dial on it stating that he was wanted for murder. His was a mission of exploration and discovery to seek out any flaws in the roost's security that would allow an assault on the roost by a special posse. He reported back that he could not see any way that an assault would be successful. And his conclusion was that outlaws heading for Hangman's Perch would have to be apprehended before they reached it.

Mindful of that report, Sam Hanley spurred his horse on. But he had not chosen wisely. What had seemed a spritely beast back in Brodie Creek, was now flagging and falling further behind. And with every passing second, Ellie was getting further away.

When he reached the rough terrain of the foothills, the mare would struggle badly. And he saw no chance at all that the horse would be in any condition to climb the steep trails higher up the mountains; trails on which he could cross paths with men, many of whom would recognize him and take pleasure in killing him.

For years those men had had to give Brodie Creek a wide berth to avoid clashing with its tough law enforcer, and that had made for longer rides and sore butts. Memories were long held, and gripes even longer still.

Given the chance, revenge would be taken and no mercy shown.

*   *   *

On reaching the foothills, Thad Cross drew rein. 'You stay put,' he ordered Ellie. 'Try and run and I'll cut you down.' He took his rifle from its saddle scabbard and climbed to higher ground to check on his backtrail. It did not surprise him any to see a rider coming hard and fast. 'Looks like that man of yours is really determined to get you back,' he called down to Ellie.

Ellie Hanley's emotions were mixed. She was pleased to think that Sam would risk everything to rescue her, and fearful that because of his trying she would lose him. She had heard many stories since she had come to Brodie Creek about the dangerous men who rode the mountain trails, and their notorious destination — the outlaw roost called Hangman's Perch. She was also aware that a lot of those men had scores to settle with Sam, and were he now to fall into their hands they would settle them in full.

'Ya know, I could just sit here and wait for your man to come into my sights,' Cross told Ellie. 'But I figure that in this neck of the woods, there's a whole pile of fellas who would want to come face to face with Marshal Sam Hanley.'

He scrambled back down from the higher ground, chuckling.

'Now, I wouldn't want to spoil their

fun none. Delivering up Sam Hanley is going to make me real pop'lar in the roost.' He scratched his stubbled chin and looked Ellie up and down. 'And I reckon those gal-hungry gents will enjoy his wife, too.' His chuckle turned to an evil sneer. 'At a price, of course. Yes, siree. I'm going to be a real pop'lar fella.'

Ellie slapped away his groping hands.

'You won't be uppity for long,' the gang-leader snarled. 'There's never less than twenty men in Hangman's Perch, honey. Sometimes double that.' He grabbed hold of her and pressed against her. 'Now, how about a little kiss, huh?'

Ellie gagged as his stinking breath filled her mouth and throat, his greasy tongue probing. She kicked him on the shins and he danced back, his face ugly with anger. He stood looking at her, clearly at a crossroads.

Then he grinned.

'You're a fighter. And I sure do like a fighter. Mount up!' He swung into the saddle and rode ahead of Ellie. A short distance on, he drew rein and turned in his saddle. 'No tricks, understood?' Then he rode on up the meandering trail, the gap between him and Hanley growing wider by the second.

13

'Come on horse,' Hanley coaxed the flagging mare, hoping that the horse would respond, but really knowing that the mare was tuckered out and only minutes away from folding if he continued to push her as hard as he had been. The horse's breathing was rapid and getting more shallow by the second, forcing him to ease off to an amble to give the beast a fighting chance of regaining her wind.

Sam Hanley looked to the foothills, not far off but still too distant. The mare coughed. He dismounted and walked the horse, his heart stricken with fear for Ellie, any hope of catching up with Thad Cross before he reached the safety of Hangman's Perch now, barring a miracle, gone.

When his spirits were at their lowest, he heard a jingle in the scrub not far away from where he was. Seconds later an old-timer riding a mule with a pack-mule in tow loaded with the implements of the prospector's trade put in an appearance. On seeing Hanley, the grizzled old man came up short. His 'Howdy,' was measured, and he was obviously unsure of the nature of the man he had come across. His caution was well-founded. He had been searching for gold in the mountains for a long time (never finding any, but still hoping and certain that it was there to be found) and knew well the kind of ugly two-legged critter a man could cross paths with if his luck was out. He had seen the stranger before, but he could not recall where. But whoever he was, at the back of his mind, the old-timer had an idea that he was a no-nonsense sort of fella. Maybe it was in the mountains he had come across him, probably on route to Hangman's Perch. And if that were so, he was talking to a man who was as dangerous as a rattler in a man's pocket.

'Howdy, friend,' Hanley greeted the grizzled old-timer, looking disappointedly at the pair of mules and wishing they were horses.

There was genuine friendliness in the stranger's manner and the old man thawed some, but he still remained watchful for any tricks on the stranger's part. Some of the badmen he had encountered in his time in the mountains had been the most affable of critters, right up to the time they shed their sheep's clothing and showed the wolf underneath.

'Your horse looks done for,' the prospector observed.

'That she is,' Hanley confirmed.

The grizzled old-timer looked about him. 'Long way from nowhere to be without a horse?'

The way he had said his words struck a chord with Hanley.

'Know where a man could get fresh horseflesh round these parts?' he enquired with cautious hope.

'Mebbe.'

The trading had begun.

'Know a place?' Sam Hanley enquired.

'Mebbe.'

Hanley took a roll of bills from his trousers pocket that made the old man's eyes light up. 'How much do you reckon it would take to refresh your memory, old-timer?' Having given him a glimpse of the roll, Hanley now shielded it from view and stepped back a couple of paces as the prospector edged closer in an attempt to judge the thickness of the roll and the denomination of the bills. The old man might be long on the tooth, but that did not mean that he could not pull a trigger or sling a knife. And, Hanley reckoned that, after a lifetime in the mountains rubbing shoulders with the scum of the territory and beyond, he might very well have picked up their tricks and their ways. He temptingly peeled off a bill.

'Now where would this place be, old-timer?'

The old man took off his battered hat

and scratched his head of scraggy hair. 'Gee, mister,' he sighed, his eyes firmly on the roll of bills, 'guess my mind ain't what it used to be.'

With no time for haggling, Hanley was tempted to ask him to state his price, but that would make the prospector aware of his urgency to get in the saddle, which would result in a hiking of the old man's greed. So he flicked another bill to add to the first. The old-timer tried to remain unconcerned, but the glint in his eyes betrayed his inner feelings. Sam Hanley flicked a third bill.

'Now, friend,' he said sternly, 'if you can't recall now, I figure I'm wasting my time parleying with a man who doesn't even know his own name.' The prospector did not comment. Hanley could see that he was trying to decide whether he could push for more. 'I guess we can't do business,' Hanley said, as if he had not a care in the world. 'I'll just rest up this nag of mine for a spell.'

'Ain't country to be restin' in,' said the old man. 'Too many *hombres* round who'd slit your throat for a rusty dime.'

Hanley settled the gun on his hip. 'I'll take my chances, mister.'

He was walking away when the old man piped up, 'For another ten dollars I'll show you the way.'

Hanley turned and made it look as though he was going to haggle, but he shrugged philosophically. 'What the heck,' he said, 'One good hand of blackjack will make good what I'll be down.' He handed over the bills to the old man. 'How far is this place?'

''Tain't far,' the old-timer said, pocketing the money and leading off. 'Now ya got to understand that Jack Sullivan's nags ain't the finest horse-flesh round. But I figure one will get ya clear of this country.' He pointed to the mountains. 'Unless you're headed for Hangman's Perch, o' course.'

'Where I'm headed is my business,' Sam Hanley replied curtly.

'Ain't pryin' none, mister,' said the

old-timer, quick to repair any offence. He had suddenly recalled where he had seen the man before — in Brodie Creek, where he toted the marshal's badge. The realization opened up another possible avenue of adding to the dollars in his pocket. The devil's spawn up in Hangman's Perch would pay good money for the kind of information he would bring them. And with his knowledge of the mountains, he could reach the outlaw roost long before the Brodie Creek lawman. But if he chose to follow that plan, he risked ending up with nothing at all, even breath. Because he was certain that if he tried to betray Sam Hanley, he'd kill him.

But it surely was a temptation to take Hanley's dollars and also to try and add the outlaws' money to his bounty.

He had seen a rider with a woman in tow a while back, whom he knew to be the evil bastard Thad Cross, and she looked none too happy to be sharing his company. And he guessed that it was fear for the woman's safety that had brought Hanley looking. And if that were so, Cross being worse than most in Hangman's Perch, his conscience, what little he had left, would have a hell of a time dealing with selling out the woman. Because that would be the result, if he sold out Hanley. However, temptation was temptation.

Made shrewd and instinctive by the long years of bullet dodging and trouble-busting, Sam Hanley could read the old-timer like an open book. He would have to watch him every step of the way.

'Frank Lombard's the name,' the old-timer said.

A short time later, though to Sam it seemed an age, Lombard led the way into a narrow canyon. Uneasy with the terrain, Hanley fell back to give him time to react, should the old man get up to any trickery. He had of neccesity shown him the roll of bills, and by having to do so to get the old man's co-operation, he had placed temptation before him. Just because he was old was no reason to trust Lombard. Temptation did not vanish with age. In fact the sense of time running out often made temptation all the more urgent to act on, as the chance presented might be the last opportunity a man would get.

Sensing Hanley falling back, the old-timer turned round. 'Ain't scared of an old-timer like me, are ya, mister?'

'While that heart is pumping blood, I figure thoughts will be in your head, Lombard,' Hanley stated bluntly.

The prospector cackled. 'You're surely a distrusting kinda gent.'

'Distrust is what's kept me alive to now,' said the former marshal of Brodie Creek.

'Jack Sullivan's place is just at the end of the canyon,' the old-timer informed Hanley. 'Now there's a critter a man wouldn't want to turn his back on.'

'A *friend* of yours?'

'Yeah. We go some way back, Jack and me.'

The old-timer's proud boast did nothing to calm Sam Hanley's increasing unease as they progressed deeper into the canyon which got narrower as they went until they reached a point where there was barely enough room for them to squeeze past.

'Tight fit, ain't it,' said the prospector.

'Doesn't seem to be an opening ahead,' Hanley observed. 'Not exactly the place for a horse trader to do business. Unlikely that anyone would find him to do business with.'

'Well, ya see, the men Jack does business with know how to find him. And other than them, Jack ain't the kinda feller who rolls out the carpet for visitors. If ya get my drift?'

Sam Hanley slowed his progress a little more.

'Don't ya fret none,' said Lombard, the mischievous glint in his eyes a sure sign of his enjoyment at Hanley's unease. 'Just a spit up ahead the trail widens out to the shape of a pregnant woman's belly. It's a small valley, but it's got the sweetest grass you ever did see. And from Jack's point of view, the thing is, if you get in and you ain't welcome,' he cackled again, showing toothless gums, 'you darn well ain't comin' out, for sure. Now that's why, in a coupla minutes, I gotta holler.'

'Holler?' Hanley questioned suspiciously.

'To let Jack know I'm comin',' the prospector explained. And when Hanley remained doubtful, he added, 'Ride in unannounced and Jack will shoot ya on sight.'

Sam Hanley was acutely aware that the old-timer's holler could have a more sinister purpose, like alerting the horse-trader to be ready to drop whoever was with the old man, but there was nothing he could do if he wanted to get a fresh horse under him but trust Frank Lombard.

'Jack!' The prospector's lungs were certainly in better shape than the rest of him. 'It's Frank Lombard come to visit.

Bringin' a friend to trade. Now we wait,' he told Hanley.

Almost immediately a single rifle shot rang out.

'That means Jack's home and he's of a welcomin' frame of mind,' Lombard explained.

As predicted, after the final breathless stretch of trail when the movement of the canyon walls by a sliver would have crushed both men, they arrived in a clearing from which a valley with lush grass, home to a remuda of contentedly grazing horses, spread out.

'Like leavin' purgatory and arrivin' in heaven, ain't it?' said Lombard.

A cabin stood to the right of the entrance where the canyon wall curved, hiding it from immediate view, giving the man standing on its porch, rifle at the ready, timely sight of any visitor.

'Howdy, Jack,' Lombard greeted the horse trader enthusiastically. 'Been a spell since my last visit.'

Sullivan did not return the old-timer's greeting. 'Who's he?' was his blunt, unfriendly question.

'A friend and customer, Jack,' said the prospector.

'The customer bit is dandy,' was Sullivan's stony reply. 'Don't know if I'd want the kind of friend you'd have round the place, Lombard.'

Frank Lombard chuckled, apparently taking no offence, but to Sam Hanley the slight stiffening of his shoulders told him that the old-timer was not as immune to Sullivan's sneering remark as he'd have one believe.

'His horse is tuckered out. Needs another,' Lombard said. 'Can afford the best, too.'

Jack Sullivan's interest perked up.

'Got some real nice horseflesh, mister,' Sullivan said, letting the rifle drop to his side as he came from the porch. 'Stallion or mare?'

'Mare,' Hanley said.

'A stallion would have a lot more grit, if it's the mountains you'll be ridin' in.'

The former marshal of Brodie Creek

did not deny or confirm his destination. 'More stubborn of nature, too, friend.'

Sullivan shrugged. 'Tradin' the wind-bag?'

'No good to me.'

Jack Sullivan considered the jaded mare. 'Hair's breadth from foldin',' was his opinion. 'Ain't worth much. Pure vulture bait.'

'Rest and feed and she'll be perky again.'

'A coupla dollars, that's all she's worth.'

'Show me the right horse, and I don't think we'll need to argue about the mare.'

Ten minutes later, Sam Hanley had made his choice, agreed an over-the-odds price and paid it.

'Nice doin' business with a man who knows his own mind,' Sullivan said. 'Anythin' else I can do for ya?' The horse-trader's eyes were greedily on Hanley's roll of bills.

'You can tell me the shortest route to Hangman's Perch.'

'In these parts, information costs,' Sullivan said, and added, 'Plenty. A whole pile of trails will get ya there. Not a whole lotta difference 'tween 'em. Except,' greed glinted in his eyes, 'one that comes to mind that'll get you there in less than half the time.'

Sullivan's expression became vague.

'If'n I can recall, that is.'

'Loss of memory is surely a heck of a big problem round these parts,' Hanley grumbled. 'How much will it take to restore *your* memory, Sullivan?'

'How much d'ya figure?'

'Not as much as you figure,' Hanley replied. 'Fifty dollars tops.'

'Hundred.'

'Sixty-five. Not a cent more.'

'I reckon you want to get to Hangman's Perch real fast,' Sullivan said. 'Eighty-five.'

'Seventy-five.'

When the horse-trader dallied further, Sam Hanley pocketed his poke.

'I'll take it,' the old-timer piped up. 'Know a real short cut, too.'

'Shuddup, you old fart!' Jack Sullivan bellowed.

'You've got yourself a deal,' Hanley said. The prospector held out his gnarled hand in which Hanley placed twenty dollars. 'You get the rest when we reach the roost.'

'Ain't fair,' Lombard complained.

'It's the only deal on offer,' Hanley barked. 'Are you taking it?'

'I'm takin' it.' Lombard shoved the twenty dollars in his pocket. 'Let's make tracks.'

'On a mule?'

'All I got, mister,' the prospector complained. 'When you get into the mountains, ain't nothin' like a mule to climb. And,' he lovingly patted the mule, 'Sarah Jane here knows these mountains better than even me.'

'Sarah Jane,' Hanley chuckled.

'Named her after a woman I near married in Dodge.' He scratched under his right armpit. 'A widow woman.' His eyes filled with loneliness of memories that, had he made another decision, might not be just memories. He looked reflectively to the mountains. 'Should have, too, I reckon,' he said, with an ocean of regret.

'How long will it take to reach Hangman's Perch?' the former marshal enquired.

'An hour — hour and a half mebbe.'

'Try and make it less. Let's ride, friend.'

'You mind my pack-mule, Jack?' Lombard asked.

'Yeah,' he snarled. 'For twenty dollars.'

'You're a thievin' whore's spit, Jack Sullivan!' the prospector ranted.

Rather than risk further delay due to haggling, Hanley handed over twenty dollars to the horse-trader.

'Now, let's get moving,' he ordered Lombard.

Sullivan's eyes fixed greedily on Hanley's roll of bills. Anticipating trouble, the former lawman was ready for it when it came. The knife appeared from up the horse-trader's sleeve as if by magic. Hanley shot him right between the eyes.

Lombard leapt from the mule and spat in Jack Sullivan's face. Then he robbed the horse-trader. 'He don't have any use for money no more,' he reasoned, conscious of Sam Hanley's scrutiny.

'Ain't none of my affair,' Hanley answered curtly. 'Let's ride.'

Lombard remounted and led off at a surprisingly quick pace for a mule. Riding up through the foothills, Sam Hanley reckoned that he would have to keep a keen eye on the old man. He had no doubt that, given the opportunity, Lombard would rob his pockets as well.

14

'Keep up!' Thad Cross growled as, exhausted, Ellie fell back. 'Fancy living's made you soft.' He sneered. 'A spell in the roost will soon fix that.'

'Can't we rest?' she pleaded.

'You can rest all you like in the roost. Well,' he sneered, 'not all that much, I guess.'

'Given the chance, I'll kill you,' Ellie vowed.

'You won't get the chance. Neither will that man of yours come anyway near rescuing you. So put any high-falutin' notions out of that pretty head of yours. Once I tire of you, and I tire easy, you'll be a working woman.'

'May you rot in hell, Cross!'

'I figure there's little doubt that I will. I reckon I had Satan's mark on me right from the second I left my momma's womb. Now keep up. I won't tell you again, woman!' Cross dug his spurs in bad-temperedly, paining his horse. 'Don't you start moaning too, horse,' he growled, and repeated the exercise with even more spite.

He was anxious to reach Hangman's Perch. A while before he had checked his backtrail and had been surprised to see the amount of progress Hanley had made. He figured that the old-timer guiding him was Frank Lombard, a prospector who knew every inch of the mountains better than the lines on the palm of his hands. He'd know trails that most men knew nothing about. And Cross worried now that the former marshal of Brodie Creek would catch him up before he reached the safety of the roost, where help would not be in short supply.

He had had one run in with Sam Hanley, which he had lost. He was not anxious for a second encounter with him. Not in the black mood Hanley would be in after he had kidnapped his wife of less than an hour.

Sam Hanley was astounded by the progress Lombard had made. The criss-cross of trails he was using did not make much sense to him, but the evidence of their worth was clear in the distance they had covered. He was beginning to hope that they could catch up with Thad Cross and Ellie before the outlaw reached the roost, until Lombard said:

'Got to rest a spell, Hanley.' The old-timer had called him Hanley. Lombard, immediately spotting his mistake, grinned. 'Recalled your name back at Sullivan's place.' He looked closely at Sam. 'Saw a rider with a woman in tow just before I crossed paths with you — Thad Cross. Him the *hombre* you're after?'

'The woman is my wife,' Sam said glumly.

'Holy shit!' Lombard exploded. 'How did Cross get his hands on your wife?'

'It's a long story that I haven't got

time to waste telling,' Hanley barked. 'We must go on.'

'Sarah Jane's all tuckered out. She ain't young no more. Got to take it slower, even when we do get started again.'

'Leave her.'

'What?'

'You heard. This mare is strong and has got good wind. We'll double up. Collect Sarah Jane on the way back.'

'I ain't leavin' my mule, Hanley,' he groused. 'We've been partners for a long time in these mountains.'

'You'll be partners again, soon as I deal with Thad Cross.'

'There ain't no dealin' with Cross. He's fast and he's mean. Most fellas up in the roost give him a wide berth when he comes a-callin'.'

Sam Hanley took the roll of bills from his pocket and held it out to Lombard. 'Every dollar is yours, if I catch up with Cross.'

The old-timer's eyes lit up. 'Every dollar?'

'Every dollar,' Hanley confirmed.

Frank Lombard's initial enthusiasm faded quickly. 'Ain't none too keen on leavin' Sarah Jane, mister,' he said, genuinely troubled for the mule's welfare.

Hanley had not given Lombard much credit. But the tussle he was having with himself now showed that there was some good in him.

'I can't pass up a chance like this, Sarah Jane,' he said. 'That roll of bills will give you and me a comfortable winter, gal. You, nice clean straw to lie in, and the best oats for your belly. Me, a feather bed, a bottle of whiskey, and a woman to pleasure me.'

The mule snorted.

'I knowed you'd understand, Sarah Jane,' he said. 'I'll be back 'fore you know I'm gone.'

When he was ready to become Hanley's saddle partner, the former marshal dismounted. 'Got to search you, Lombard. You'll be riding behind me.'

172

'You don't trust me?' the old-timer asked, with wide-eyed innocence.

'No.'

Lombard laughed. 'Right, too, Mr Hanley. Me, I wouldn't trust nobody.'

'Seems sensible, with the company you keep.'

The old-timer held out his arms. 'Search all you like,' he invited Hanley. 'Only don't fall in love with me, huh.'

The search yielded up a stiletto and a derringer, the stiletto evidently recently used judging by the dried blood on its blade.

'A man's got to do what's needed in this rough-house territory,' said the old-timer. 'There's critters round here that would cut your throat for a plate of beans.'

'Did you enjoy the beans, Lombard?'

The old man cackled. 'Every darn one, Hanley.'

Sam Hanley mounted up and gave Lombard a hand up. 'Just one thing, Lombard,' he said, before starting out. 'I'll kill you, before you kill me.'

The prospector held Sam Hanley's gaze. 'You know, Hanley, when it comes down to it, we ain't all that diff'rent.'

'Men have been killed for lesser insults than that,' Hanley said. 'Giddup, horse.'

★   ★   ★

Scanning his backtrail again Cross found Hanley and Lombard, even doubled up in the saddle, much closer than he expected them to be. The outlaw's face clouded with worry.

★   ★   ★

Following Lombard's directions, and hoping that he was not being walked into a trap, Sam Hanley climbed steadily upwards until the prospector told him to draw rein.

'This is as far as we go on horseback, Hanley,' he said.

'There's still a lot of trail to cover,' the former marshal of Brodie Creek observed, looking to the summit to Hangman's Perch, the view from which was all-commanding. It was known that the roost always had a look-out, so how had they come so far without being spotted and an exploratory party sent out to intercept the strangers?

'Hangman's Perch has got a blind spot,' Lombard explained, when Hanley put that question to him. 'To the south of the entrance to the roost there's this rock, long and tall and as pointed as a needle that cuts off the look-out's view. We've been travellin' along a route that's in line with that blind spot. And that's why we ain't heard nothin' from the roost, friend.'

The old-timer's explanation sounded as mossy as an Irish bog. Was Lombard spinning him a yarn? Tagging him along until he walked him into a trap? It might seem proud and big-headed, but there were a lot of men in Hangman's Perch who would pay top dollar to get their hands on a lawman who, if they dared show their face in Brodie Creek, would run them out. And more men still whose butts had been made raw by the longer ride forced on them to reach the roost, having to give Brodie Creek a wide berth.

'When you hired Frank Lombard as your guide, you hired the darn best there is,' the old-timer boasted. 'Know every nook and cranny in these mountains. I've been over and under them a million times in the thirty years I've been searchin' for gold.'

'Everyone knows there isn't any gold in these mountains,' Hanley said.

'Hah! Ain't so.' Lombard's eyes shone with a fevered intensity. 'I just know there's gold in this pile of rock, Hanley. Can feel it in my bones.'

'Thirty years is a long time to be feeling with nothing to show.'

'Only a matter of time,' the prospector said, cockily confident.' He sniffed the air. 'Winter's at our door now. But I'll be back again come spring. Meanwhile that roll of bills you'll be handin' over will keep me and Sarah Jane cosy.

'Now start examining the horse's leg, and act like it's big trouble.'

'What for?'

'Just do it. It's got a point to it.' Sam Hanley did as he was told. 'Now when you straighten up act like you're mad as hell. Then you'll pretend to tell me your woes, and I'll join in. Got that, friend?'

A couple of moments later Hanley straightened up, and stalked about like a man whose luck had just deserted him. He remonstrated with Lombard who, in turn, joined in the mime. After a couple of minutes of play-acting, the old-timer said:

'We can stop now.'

'What were we doing it for in the first place?' Hanley wanted to know.

'To convince that *hombre* whose got your woman that we had big problems, of course.'

'You saw him?'

'Nope.'

'Then what in tarnation are you on about?'

'Directly above there's a turn in the

final leg of the trail into Hangman's Perch. Ev'ry hardcase I've known has stopped there to check his backtrail. Second nature to men who seek out the roost. Like looking into your backyard at night to make sure your hen house is safe, before you close the door.'

Sam Hanley shot the prospector a sceptical look.

'Heard that you're as tough as rusty nails to eat back in Brodie Creek,' Lombard went on. 'Takes a special kinda man to ramrod a town. But up here in the mountains, it takes another kind; the kind of man who knows the way of birds and creatures and what it means when they act different. And a man who can think like the mountain's natural inhabitants, sensing danger when there's not a sign of it to see. Listen, friend,' he encouraged Hanley.

'For what? There's nothing to hear.'

'Sure there ain't. But that ain't natural.'

★　★　★

Higher up Thad Cross was laughing. He climbed down from the rocks from where he had been checking his backtrail, before completing the last mile or so to Hangman's Perch.

'What's so funny?' Ellie questioned him.

'Looks like your man's got nag trouble. I guess him and that old bastard are stranded.'

On hearing Cross's news, Ellie was utterly crest-fallen. She had lived in the hope that Sam would catch her up while the odds on him rescuing her from Cross's clutches were even, if not a little in his favour. However, once Cross reached Hangman's Perch and the protection of his fellow cut-throats there would be nothing Sam could do, except throw away his life in a vain attempt to breach the roost's defences.

'Maybc you'll get some sense in that pretty head of yours now and see the sense of co-operating.'

Ellie Hanley contemptuously spat in Cross's face as he tried to kiss her.

Rattler mean, he struck out, laying the back of his hand across the side of Ellie's head to send her flying back to crash against a tree with enough force to rattle her insides. A dark cloud swept over her, and her surroundings spun dizzily. She fell forward. Cross caught her. 'Now we wouldn't want that pretty face all busted up, would we?' He snorted. 'A man pays a lot more for a pretty woman than he would for one with a battered face.'

He hauled Ellie to her feet and shoved her roughly towards her horse. Her anger, sweeping back, she drew her nails across the outlaw's right cheek. He made to strike her again, but held back.

'I can wait to kill you, woman,' he said, fighting his wrath. 'And I will,' he promised. 'But not before you're an old dried-up hag.' He laughed meanly. 'With all those woman-starved critters up in the roost, it shouldn't take too long.' He cast his eyes up towards Hangman's Perch. 'And nights are real long.'

Ellie tried to grab his sixgun, but he shoved her away.

'Don't know whether you wanted to shoot me or yourself. But either, I figure, would sure be a darn waste. Now it's time we made tracks. Ain't far. So you relax and look your prettiest when we ride in.'

★　★　★

'How long do we have to keep this play-acting up, Lombard?' Sam Hanley asked impatiently.

' 'Til that critter, who I'm certain is watchin' us, is satisfied that your horse is done for and we are too. A man might as well be without his legs as a horse in this neck of the woods.'

'Can we cut Cross off before he reaches Hangman's Perch?'

'Reckon so. I know me a short cut that'll put you ahead of him.'

'Then let's move.'

'Don't be a fool,' the old-timer barked. 'You know better than to go jumpin' in.'

'That's my wife Cross has got,' the former marshal of Brodie Creek growled. 'And there's a whole pile of skirt-hungry men up in that roost. At least if I'm dead, I won't have to live thinking every day about what Ellie's going through.

'So you show me this short-cut to that outlaws' hell-hole right now. Or,' he drew his sixgun, 'I'll cut you down like a weed in a field of corn, Lombard.'

The old man looked at Hanley steadily, unafraid. 'Hanley, I've been close to death too many times to worry about bein' close to it again. So stop wavin' that damn pistol 'bout. This way.' He led the way through dense brush and scrub into a solid wall of rock.

'What game are you playing, Lombard?' Sam growled.

'Ya know, you're a real impatient fella, Hanley. Just go where I go.'

Lombard vanished through a narrow aperture in the rock. Hanley followed, and found himself inside a pitch-dark

182

cave full of slithering sounds.

'Snakes,' Lombard said. 'Been round them all my natural. If you don't trouble them, they won't trouble you none.'

Sam Hanley wished that he could believe Lombard, but try as he might his blood still ran as cold as Yukon ice.

The grizzled prospector walked ahead as if he was walking down the main street of Brodie Creek.

'Wait up,' Hanley summoned. 'What if what you say is all hooey, Lombard, and the snakes don't scare as easy as you say?'

The old-timer chuckled.

'Then it ain't goin' to worry you none after that first nip, is it? Now, that fella you're figurin' on settlin' accounts with is gettin' nearer to Hangman's Perch every second you delay.'

On Lombard's reminder, Sam Hanley forgot about the danger to himself and strode forward. 'Where does this lead,' he asked, as the opening of the cave led to a narrow, low-ceilinged passage that dipped lower still before it climbed steadily upwards.

'It's been a heck of a time since I've been in this cave,' Lombard said. 'But if I'm reckonin' right, you'll be waitin' on the blind side of a spot called snake bend, so called because of its twisting nature, for Cross to show.'

'And if you haven't got your reckoning right?' Hanley enquired.

'Then you can shoot me,' Lombard stated flatly.

'I will,' the former marshal of Brodie Creek promised.

As they progressed ever deeper into the cave, Lombard warned, 'Whatever you do, don't start no shootin' till you see clear daylight. Lots of gases in here that will blow you right through the roof of this rock.'

The old-timer led on.

'Air gets thin, too,' he added. 'And what little is left gets foul pretty quick. So we ain't got time for no more speechifying or dallying, Hanley.'

Ten minutes later a sudden shaft of light, just like the light of a divine presence, shone down from above and a welcome breeze chased away the stench of foul air.

Lombard looked up. 'Sure hope that the rope ladder I slung down here a coupla years ago ain't rotted 'way.'

'Rope ladder!' Hanley yelped.

'Only way outta here,' Lombard said, pointing to the hole through which the light was entering the cave atop a sheer rockface that was as smooth as a baldman's head. 'Yeah,' he enthused. 'There's that ladder. Shorter than I figured though. Critters prob'ly chewing on it. C'mere. I'll give ya a leg up, Hanley. Should be able to reach the ladder then.'

'Once I'm on the ladder, I'll pull you up.'

'No you won't. That ladder won't bear the weight of two of us. It'll snap and we'll both be stranded down here. I'll make my way back through the cave.'

Sam Hanley was instantly suspicious. 'And leave me to have my head blown off the second I poke it through that hole up there. Then you'll collect for delivering me up. That your plan, Lombard?'

Frank Lombard's face suffused with anger.

'I know I don't stand high in your reckonin' of what a man should be, Hanley,' he fumed. 'And I admit that a time or two I thought about collectin' on your head. But I figured you treated me fair, so I'm treatin' you fair, too. Besides, that no-good Thad Cross shot my partner a coupla years ago, for no good reason other than he was of a mind to at the time.'

He took the money Hanley had given him from his pocket and offered it back to the former marshal.

'Take it. Only thing I want is to see Cross get hot lead in the gut.'

'You keep it, Lombard,' Hanley said, convinced of the old-timer's sincerity. 'And,' he took from his pocket his bank-roll and handed it over, 'You head back to Brodie Creek. I'll be along shortly to slake our thirst, friend.'

Lombard took the money.

'I ain't had many words with the Lord these past times, Hanley,' he said. 'But if he still wants to listen, I'll have something to say as I make my way back along.'

'Thanks. I'll need all the help I can get.'

With Lombard's help Sam Hanley grabbed hold of the ragged rope ladder and prayed that it would be strong enough to hold his full weight when he climbed on to it. He dared not breathe as he tested the ladder. Below him, he could sense Lombard's tension, too. The ladder felt powdery. Several strands of the frayed rope drifted past him, featherlike. He could smell the decay. He reached out with his other hand to grab the ladder, acutely conscious that the stress on the crumbling rope would be doubled.

Would that be too much for the rope ladder to bear?

15

Hanley felt the rope ladder shudder as it swayed under his full weight.

'Don't fight it,' was Lombard's advice. 'Be patient and it will find its own settling point.'

The former marshal of Brodie Creek knew the wisdom of the old prospector's advice, but he had to fight hard to overcome the urge to scramble up the ladder before it shredded and pitched him back into the cave, all hope of reaching Ellie gone. As the ladder swayed from side to side, Sam collided painfully with the rockface. He forced himself to measure his climb. Slowly the ladder began to settle. Almost every rung on the rope ladder disintegrated the second his foot left it, and the creaking of the rope sounded ever more strained.

★　★　★

Ellie Hanley's hope was fast fading, while Thad Cross's confidence grew, certain now that there was no way that Sam Hanley could make up ground. In a short while they would be inside the fortress that was Hangman's Perch and she hoped that Sam would not then try to rescue her, because it would mean certain death for him. And, anyway, once inside the outlaw roost with what Thad Cross had in mind for her, she would not want to be rescued. Because from then on she would have nothing to offer a decent man.

'Looks like the gods ain't with ya, darlin',' Cross mocked Ellie.

'Damn you to hell, Cross!'

He laughed. 'Well,' his finger pointed upwards, 'you might say that I sure as hell won't be going that a-way, honey.'

* * *

Hand over hand, Sam Hanley clawed his way up the rope ladder feeling the bite of the rope and the graze of the rockface as each movement brought him into contact with the rock. But driven by the need to rescue his wife, he forced the pain from his mind and went on doggedly upwards. His next worry was, would he be able to squeeze through the narrow hole at the top, because the nearer he got to it the narrower it seemed to be. Lombard was on the scrawny side, while he had, of late, put on some extra pounds due to partaking of Ellie's scrumptious cooking. It would be one hell of an irony if, now, those dinners under his belt were to impede his rescue of Ellie.

Though he had thought of it, Lombard had not mentioned that very possibility, figuring at the time that Hanley had enough to worry about without him adding to his concerns. But looking up now, and seeing Sam Hanley nearing the hole and blocking out its light, he could see that if the former marshal did squeeze through, it would be by the narrowest of margins.

But the likelihood was that he would

have too much meat and muscle on him.

Up to now Frank Lombard had never worried much about any man's troubles but his own. Now he worried that by using the cave as a means to snare Thad Cross, he had chosen unwisely. Maybe he should have continued up the mountain and hoped for a lucky break to gain on Cross. But his experience of luck had been that when you needed her most, the lady became fickle. He comforted himself with the thought that if Hanley did not reach his wife on time, his bad fortune had started back when the former marshal's horse had run out of spit.

Sam Hanley sucked in every smidgen of his bulk to squeeze through the hole at the top of the cave. It was still a tight fit, and he had to sacrifice some skin to make it through, but when he sucked fresh air his spirits soared. And went even higher still on catching sight of Thad Cross and Ellie lower down the winding trail.

A sharp twist in the trail hid him from view and gave him the element of surprise. Hanley knew that he had a lot to be grateful to Lombard for, because he had chosen well the ambush location from which he would launch his attack on Cross.

Now all he had to do was plan that attack. So close to the outlaw roost, gunfire was out. He'd use a knife, but for some unfathomable reason he had never mastered the art of slinging a blade; an art he believed a man could learn poorly but really had to be born with for real skill. So with a gun and knife out of the question, what was he left with? Hanley racked his brain for a solution to his problem, and then it came to him. He ripped the sleeve off his shirt and used it to make a garrotte. Used properly and with timeliness, it would be as deadly as any gun or knife.

Makeshift garrotte prepared, Hanley climbed up through the trailside boulders above the trail and crouched down to await Cross's arrival.

16

Sam Hanley's breath caught in his throat when Cross drew rein, ears cocked, eyes alert. Had he heard something? A couple of pebbles of shale maybe? The scrape of a boot-heel? The rip of cloth when he had torn the sleeve from his shirt to make a garrotte? He had moved as silently as he could, lawmen moving with stealth was a craft learned early. Cross might not have heard a thing. Perhaps the outlaw's instincts had kicked in, and he was sensing rather than having any clear evidence of trouble.

Cross looked to his right to a snaking trail that would eventually reach Hangman's Perch but not as quickly as the direct route he was on. And the trail, barely wide enough to accommodate a single rider, perilously hugged the side of the mountain. Cross would have to measure every step. The outlaw's consideration of the hazardous trail was, for Sam, a new worry. Because where Cross went Ellie would have to follow, and she was in no way an experienced enough rider for that.

Sam Hanley got ready to show himself if Cross opted for the new trail. He would throw away his advantage and it would mean gunfire, which would mean that he and Ellie would probably never get off the mountain. But he could see no other way out of his dilemma. He was ready to spring to his feet to challenge Cross when the outlaw ruled out the more precipitous trail and continued along the trail he was on, his easy gait in the saddle a sign that he had discounted his concerns.

Ellie Hanley breathed again. She had the shivery feeling that she got when ever Sam was near, but unseen. She was certain he was close by. The first time Sam had come up behind her in Brodie Creek she had keenly sensed his presence, and ever since she had known he was around even before she set eyes on him.

'Ain't much I'll be able to do without you knowing about it, Ellie,' Sam had joked about her ability to turn just as he put in an appearance. 'But I'm sure glad I've got under your skin like I have,' he had added.

But where exactly was Sam lurking? She hoped that the shivery thrill Sam's nearness sent through her back in Brodie Creek would still work in less civilized surroundings. If it did, she might just have a couple of seconds to help Sam overcome Thad Cross.

*　*　*

Sam Hanley knew he had to judge his leap on to Cross, inch perfect A trifle mistimed and he'd crash on to the stony trail and Cross would kill him instantly. His legs ached with the tension in his muscles as he sat on his haunches, ready any second now to act. He wound the makeshift garrotte as taut as he could, wanting no slack in it that Cross could get a finger inside.

Another couple of yards and Cross would be within range.

★ ★ ★

Ellie Hanley groaned to get Cross's attention, and swayed in the saddle. Fearing she would faint and topple from her horse, he rounded — damaged goods were not half as valuable. When he saw the flash of triumph in Ellie's eyes, he knew that his earlier instincts had been right. He turned in the saddle to see Sam Hanley leaping at him.

In a second flat Hanley was on the outlaw's back, the garrotte round his neck. Cross managed to draw his gun, but it flew out of his hand as they crashed to the ground, Sam coming off worse as he had to bear Cross's weight. The gun clattered on the rocks directly above the hole down into the cave, sparked and exploded as it vanished down the hole. The ground shook under them as the gases in the cave which Lombard had warned about ignited, and a slice of the mountain crashed down into the cave. Sam was shocked, knowing that there was little hope that Frank Lombard could have survived the blast. But he had to finish Cross before worrying about the old-timer. He tightened the garrotte round the outlaw's neck with even greater purpose and anger, and with every ounce of his strength he twisted and twisted, taking comfort and pleasure too from the gagging sounds coming from the outlaw's gaping mouth.

Slowly, Thad Cross's kicking became less and less until at last his legs shot out straight and stilled. Sam Hanley loosened the garrotte and lay back, winded. Ellic threw herself on him, her lips kissing every inch of his face.

'I've got to get to Lombard,' he said, getting to his feet.

'Lombard?'

'The old prospector who showed me the way to catch up with Cross, Ellie.' He pointed to the now gaping hole, still emitting clouds of black dust and sparks. 'He's still down there.'

'Look, Sam.'

Hanley followed Ellie's line of vision to the high rocks above the entrance to Hangman's Perch, where several excited outlaws were congregated. Waiting around to try and rescue Lombard would bring company he did not want. And leaving the old-timer, probably dead, but maybe just injured, did not settle well with his conscience.

Ellie made up his mind for him.

'We'll have to try and rescue the man who helped you, Sam,' she said. 'There'd be no living with the bad feeling if we didn't.'

'We?'

'Sure. I'm not going to hang around here with a crowd of woman-hungry men piling out of Hangman's Perch. What would be the point in all of this, if that happened?'

'You know, Ellie Hanley,' Sam said. 'I married me some feisty skirt.'

'How far did you have to climb out of that hole?' she asked. She grabbed the lariat from Thad Cross's saddlehorn. 'Length of a rope do?'

'More likely two lengths,' Hanley said. He picked up his lariat, knotted the ropes together and pulled hard on the joint to tighten it as much as he could. He went and tied the rope to a nearby tree and then dropped the other end into the cave. 'Lombard, you hearing me?' he hollered, but got no reply. 'I'll go first,' he told Ellie. 'Test this rope. If anything happens to me, you mount up and ride like hell, Ellie.' He took her in his arms and kissed her passionately. Her response was equally passionate. He grinned. 'Hell, I sure hope that there'll be more of those kisses to come.'

Ellie Hanley returned her husband's grin.

'It's my intention to send you to sleep every night all tuckered out,' she said.

Laughing, Sam Hanley descended into the cave. As he dropped into the murky darkness he saw tons of rubble and figured that the decision to try and rescue Lombard had not been a wise one. There was no way he could imagine that the old man could have survived the blast. 'Lombard!' he hollered again.

He thought he heard a cough. Sam Hanley peered into the swirling clouds of dust.

'Told ya there was gold in these mountains,' Lombard said, his voice weak and breathless. Sam scrambled down to where the old man was trapped under a pile of rocks. 'Heck, don't you fret none 'bout me, Hanley. Had the lives of a cat. Don't waste your time,' he went on, as Sam began to pull away the rocks. 'Ain't no way I'm leavin' here. I'm busted up good. Don't want to, neither, Sam.'

'Don't want to?' Hanley questioned the old man.

'I'm goin' to die lookin' at gold,

Hanley,' he said. 'The way I figured I'd always like to go.' He sucked in a long, weary breath and shuddered. He opened the palm of his hand, holding a precious nugget. 'You've got your own gold waitin'. Make tracks before it'll be snatched away from you, friend.'

'I'm not leaving you here to rot,' Hanley declared.

'Damn it! Ain't you got ears to listen with? I'm where I want to be most. Now, git! Give your woman a big kiss from Frank Lombard.' He coughed and blood spilled from his lips. His eyes rolled. He kissed the nugget. 'Told ya there was gold in these hills, friend.'

His sigh summed up the long years he had spent searching for his particular treasure, and the regret that he had not found it earlier. Lombard's eyes closed for the last time.

* * *

Sam Hanley drew rein on a hill overlooking Brodie Creek and turned in the wagon seat to look back. Ellie could see a whole pile of memories in her husband's eyes. She let him be, until his memories ran their course, then she said:

'Are you absolutely sure this is what you want, Sam? Because if it isn't, there's no loss of pride in saying so. Brodie Creek will be a good place to bring up a family. Dan Cockrell will pull through, and he's told me that if you want your badge back he'll gladly fall back to deputy, if that's what you want, Sam.'

Sam Hanley looked fondly at his wife.

'I've got all I want right here beside me,' he said. 'So let's go and start that ranch, woman.'

Ellie Hanley returned his smile, her heart singing out.

'Then, husband,' she said. 'Give those horses their head.'

'You know,' Sam said, as they rolled on their way 'I figure that our firstborn, a son, of course,' Ellie's smile widened, 'should be named Frank, after Lombard. Because without him none of this happiness might have been ours.'

'That's the second great idea you've had, Sam Hanley.'

'The second?'

'Yes. The first was marrying me,' Ellie said smugly.

'I can't dispute that, wife,' he said sincerely, and kissed her.

THE END

We do hope that you have enjoyed reading this large print book.

Did you know that all of our titles are available for purchase?

We publish a wide range of high quality large print books including:
Romances, Mysteries, Classics
General Fiction
Non Fiction and Westerns

Special interest titles available in large print are:
The Little Oxford Dictionary
Music Book, Song Book
Hymn Book, Service Book

Also available from us courtesy of Oxford University Press:
Young Readers' Dictionary
(large print edition)
Young Readers' Thesaurus
(large print edition)

For further information or a free brochure, please contact us at:
Ulverscroft Large Print Books Ltd.,
The Green, Bradgate Road, Anstey,
Leicester, LE7 7FU, England.
Tel: (00 44) **0116 236 4325**
Fax: (00 44) **0116 234 0205**

MASSACRE AT BLUFF POINT

I. J. Parnham

Ethan Craig has only just started working for Sam Pringle's outfit when Ansel Stark's bandits bushwhack the men at Bluff Point. Ethan's new colleagues are gunned down in cold blood and he vows revenge. But Ethan's manhunt never gets underway — Sheriff Henry Fisher arrests him and he's accused of being a member of the very gang he'd sworn to track down! With nobody believing his innocence and a ruthless bandit to catch, can Ethan ever hope to succeed?

DEATH AT BETHESDA FALLS

Ross Morton

Jim Thorp did not relish this visit to Bethesda Falls. His old sweetheart Anna worked there and he was hunting her brother Clyde, the foreman of the M-bar-W ranch. Her brother is due to wed Ellen, the rancher's daughter. He is also poisoning the old man to hasten the inheritance. Thorp's presence in town starts the downward slide into violence . . . and danger for Anna, Ellen and Thorp himself. It is destined to end in violence and death.

VENGEANCE UNBOUND

Henry Christopher

There are some folk who brand Russell Dane a coward — some believe him to be a murderer. And Dane has many more who want him dead: the man he should have fought in a duel; his own uncle; the town that tried to lynch him, and the outlaws he takes refuge with. With so many out for his blood Dane must learn to handle a Colt and confront his enemies. Will his gun craft keep him alive . . . ?

SHOOT-OUT AT OWL CREEK

Corba Sunman

With a law star in his pocket and a gun in his holster, Kell Bannon rides into the Big Bend country of Texas to set up the Parfitt gang for capture. Prepared for a shoot-out, he faces more trouble with Clarkville's crooked Sheriff Bixby; the aggressive ranch foreman, Piercey; and Mack Jex, boss of the local rustling business. It's tough work, and for Bannon, he knows that only his deadly gun and quick shooting can bring a satisfactory result.

JUDGE COLT PRESIDES

George J. Prescott

When one of the powerful Ducane family is hanged for murder in a border town, his father wipes out the place in revenge. Deputy Federal Marshal Fargo Reilly goes south to dispense justice and becomes involved in a gun-running conspiracy, and a plot to murder the president of Mexico. Reilly and his deputy Matt Crane fight to destroy the gang. But can Reilly also stop them from ransacking the nearby town of Perdition, where *Judge Colt Presides?*